D1553194

FIC   Babson, Marian.
        Tightrope for three

$16.95

DATE			

TIGHTROPE FOR THREE

Also By Marian Babson

TIGHTROPE FOR THREE

Marian Babson

WALKER AND COMPANY
New York

Fic

With thanks to Humphrey Bishop, Ian Becket and Donald Rumbleow for technical advice and assistance.

72520262

Copyright © 1978 by Marian Babson

Published in the United States of America in 1989
by Walker Publishing Company, Inc.

Library of Congress Cataloging-in-Publication Data

Babson, Marian.
   Tightrope for three / Marian Babson.
      p.   cm.
   ISBN 0-8027-5750-2
   I. Title.
PS3552.A25T54   1989
813'.54—dc20   89-22489

Printed in the United States of America

2   4   6   8   10   9   7   5   3   1

CHAPTER I

He had been jarred awake by the first ring of the telephone. He snatched the receiver off the cradle to keep it from waking Lillian, and then got out of bed and carried the whole thing over by the window as he perceived that this was going to be a long, and probably involved, conversation. What was Harlow doing ringing at this time of night – or rather, morning?

'. . . thought you ought to know . . .' Harlow babbled nervously. 'Didn't like the sound of it at the time, and I've been thinking it over ever since, and – '

Paul Jarvis waited, not too patiently. *Dithering,* Harlow meant, not 'thinking it over'. But if he said anything, sounded too brusque or abrupt, Harlow would freeze, blurt out an apology, and ring off. It would be hours then, perhaps days, before he knew what the score was. And it had to be something vital for Harlow to take the risk of disturbing the head of the Company.

'Well, I've taken the liberty . . . I mean, I thought it would be wise – '

Get on with it! The command pulsed through his brain with such intensity that Harlow, miles away in London, must have felt seismic echoes from it.

'I've ordered up the Company helicopter.' Harlow was suddenly brisk and businesslike. 'It's on its way. It should be there within the hour. If you'll put the lights on in the tennis court – the net *is* down, isn't it?'

'It is. It's down for the season. So are the poles.

Won't be set up again until spring.'

'That's all right, then.' Harlow's sigh of relief was audible. It must have frightened him, taking all that responsibility – and what would happen to him if the helicopter should crash land? 'I thought it would be. Of course, if it wasn't, I thought of the swimming pool as a second choice, although I wasn't sure if it was big enough and – The pool *is* drained, isn't it?'

'This is Dartmoor in November,' he said. 'Naturally, the swimming pool is drained!'

'Yes . . . yes . . .' The snarl of power had raced along the lines and lashed at Harlow. 'I thought it would be. I was *sure* it would be. The tennis court, too. I mean, Dartmoor – in November!'

'That's all right.' Quickly, Paul tried to restore Harlow's confidence – he needed that if he were ever to find out what was going on. 'I'm glad you've ordered out the helicopter. Good thinking. Why?'

Why? That was the question. The question only Harlow could answer at this point. Harlow, the man with a foot in each camp – the man with a foot in *every* camp. Harlow, the human centipede. Be there a camp, a faction, a splinter group – and Harlow was there. Harlow, with a foot in the door, a ready smile of sympathy on his face, an ear quivering to listen to each complaint, each injustice, each plot. Whatever was going on, anywhere in the Company, Harlow would know about it. Everyone depended on him for information; no one trusted him. Had they all underestimated him? Was Harlow really the cleverest of them all?

'Why?' Harlow repeated. 'Oh, yes, *why?* Ha-ha. Well, er, it's rather a *delicate* situation. I mean . . .'

In his impatience, Paul Jarvis had twitched the draperies aside and was staring out into the night. He saw a light suddenly blaze in Dower House Cottage. Momentarily it distracted him and he lost the thread of what Harlow was saying. Why was life always so complicated?

'. . . thought you'd be back in Canada by now . . . the Board, I mean . . .' Harlow's voice recalled him to the immediate crisis, superseding all those preceding it. 'So, naturally . . . I mean, it seemed to them . . . the Board . . . that this was the best time to call an emergency meeting of the shareholders. Well, you know, there's been a lot of comment . . . Complaints . . . the Press – '

'I know,' he said grimly. EngAm International had liquidity problems these days. That did not make them unique among companies, but EngAm International had, perhaps, more enemies within than the usual run of companies these days – and now, it seemed, the enemies within were poised to strike.

'I've tried to get hold of Duckie,' the voice burbled on. 'Miss Duxworthy, I mean, your secretary – '

'I know who my secretary is,' he said forbiddingly. Across the room, Lillian opened her eyes, turned her head and found the next pillow vacant. She raised her head, discovered him at the telephone, and groped for her robe and slippers in the same abstracted way she groped for notepad and pencil when an informal meeting abruptly turned into something that ought to be recorded.

'But she isn't at home,' Harlow went on, only slightly daunted. Was there a slight innuendo in his tone? 'I tried her flat in town and her parents' home in the country, well, *suburbs*. But they said she was on holiday with friends.'

'That's all right,' Paul said. 'I know where she is. I'll get in touch with Miss Duxworthy myself.'

'Oh, good.' Was there the trace of a snigger behind Harlow's words? 'I knew you'd want her to be there. I mean, she knows so *much* about the inner workings of the business, doesn't she?'

'Miss Duxworthy is quite invaluable,' Paul confirmed gravely. 'I don't know what *any* of us would do without her.' Lillian had reached his side, her eyes questioning. She put her hand over his and tilted the phone so that, head-to-head, they could both listen.

'Oh, quite.' Harlow said enthusiastically. '*Quite*. Duckie, I mean, Miss Duxworthy, is practically part of the *furniture* – I mean, the beams and *rafters* of the Company. When you're in Canada all winter, the way you usually are, the rest of us would be *lost* without her.'

Lillian stuck her tongue out at the phone. Paul Jarvis grinned and tried not to let amusement show in his voice. 'I'm glad you realize that.'

'Oh, I do, I do. We *all* do. I mean – '

'What time is the Extraordinary General Meeting?' It was time to call Harlow back to order. Good practice for the meeting tomorrow. And wouldn't everyone be surprised – and disconcerted – when he put in his unscheduled appearance?

'First thing in the morning. I mean, *first* thing. Eight a.m. It's rather unusual, but they've got a quorum. And, of course, they've been collecting proxies for quite some time, as it turns out. Very quietly, of course.'

'Of course.' It was unusual, but it could be done – was being done. And the hour had been brilliantly arranged so that it could not possibly coincide with any scheduled flight from Canada or the United States. A Company jet might have made it in time, but EngAm didn't run to a Company jet right now – just a Company helicopter. Fortunately for him, but not for the plotters, that was going to be enough today.

'Well, I thought you ought to know . . . I mean, I thought you'd want to be here – '

'You were right.' It was time for the acknowledging word, the pat on the head. *Good dog.* 'When did you say the helicopter ought to get here?'

'Within the hour.' The voice was efficient again. 'I dispatched it as soon as I took the decision. Even allowing for the fog . . .' it hesitated.

'The fog isn't bad down here.' Even as he spoke, Paul saw that there was a solid layer of mist shrouding the lawn outside. His eyes had been deceived because, higher up, the night was still clear, the blackness broken only by the clear light shining reproachfully from Dower House Cottage, brighter and clearer than it might otherwise have seemed had he not been viewing it with the eyes of guilt.

'That's all right then,' Harlow said, relieved. 'An hour at the outside and the helicopter will be setting down on the tennis court . . . You won't forget to turn on the floodlights?'

'I won't forget.' Harlow might have been invaluable, if only he had ever learned to delegate, not dither; to entrust someone with a mission and then leave it to that person, not returning every ten minutes to hover and make sure the work was being done. But, give him his due – tonight he had turned up trumps.

'I won't forget you, either, Harlow.' Paul allowed warmth, approbation, to seep into his voice. EngAm would owe Harlow something for this night's work. Another step up the ladder which, Harlow being basically untrustworthy, would stop somewhere short of the top, but which would boost his eventual pension considerably.

'No, really. I felt it was my duty.' The satisfaction in Harlow's voice revealed that he had got the message. The message he had been seeking when he made the phone call. Harlow had one more message of his own to transmit. 'I *told* them they were rushing their fences, that you'd be able to sort everything out as soon as you got back. There's no good changing horses in midstream.'

Translation: Harlow didn't feel the opposing forces were strong enough to warrant joining. Not this time.

The light in Dower House Cottage seemed to dim and then regain full strength. The fog was beginning to roll in.

'That's right,' Paul said. 'I'm glad you realize it.'

'Well, naturally, I – '

'I'll begin packing.' Paul cut off the impending flow of self-justification. 'Fortunately, I've been going over the figures. I have almost everything we need right here. If you'll just get the Montreal statistics together –'

'They're all ready. I thought you'd want them.'

'Good. I'll also need – ' He continued dictating his requirements to Harlow, aware that Lillian had turned away and begun to dress quickly. He tried to keep his attention trained on Harlow, so far away in London – the man on the spot, so vital to him at this moment.

Yet, there *they* were, each on one side of his peripheral vision: Lillian, frowning now as she tugged a hairbrush through the heavy blonde tangle; and, on the other side, the quiet rebuke of the lighted window in Dower House Cottage.

The crisis was in London; there was no time to spare for the problems of his emotional life. Not even if he could isolate and put a name – regret? remorse? guilt? – to the feelings that assailed him. It was wiser, it was safer, to concentrate on the Boardroom battle shaping up in London right now.

'That's all?' Harlow enquired as he stopped. 'You're sure that will be enough?'

'That will hold them for a while,' Paul confirmed. 'We'll have time to go over the rest when I get there.' The helicopter should get them to London in plenty of time to do some fast telephoning, bring some pressure to bear, amass some forces of his own to face the opponents who were expecting no resistance. The opponents who believed him safely out of the country – as he usually was in November – and who thought it was safe to make their surprise bid to gain control. Probably they thought they had Harlow on their side. Next time they might have.

'I'll have everything ready at this end,' Harlow assured him. 'I've pulled in Denton and he's with me now, ready to work all night, if need be – '

'Good man.'

'And you say you can locate Miss Duxworthy – ' Insinuation just this side of slyness crept into Harlow's voice. 'So we ought to be able to win the day.'

'Fine.' Paul regretted the earlier words of praise. Harlow was dangerous, basically untrustworthy, and always on the winning side. But, for a little while longer, Harlow was necessary. 'I'll see you soon.'

'I'll be waiting,' Harlow said. 'I've directed the helicopter to set down on the roof – at the hour you'll arrive, there'll be no one in the City to complain – and I'll be in your office with all the papers.'

'Fine,' Paul said again. 'We'll be there.' He rang off.

'Paul?' Lillian was dressed and at his side. That was why the fatal 'we' had slipped out. He wondered if Harlow had noticed it. But that was optimism creeping in. Harlow noticed everything and stored it away to be used against one at some future date. When the tide had turned and the knowledge could make Harlow more useful to whatever new masters he had decided to throw in his lot with.

'I don't like that nasty little man.' Unconsciously, Lillian echoed his thoughts. 'I don't like him at all.'

'We don't have to like him.' Paul smiled down at her. 'At the moment, he's useful to us. That's all that need concern us.'

'I suppose you're right.' Lillian's arm encircled his waist. They turned away from the window.

As they turned, a second window flared a distress signal of light into the night from Dower House Cottage.

CHAPTER II

She was asleep and yet she was not asleep. She was dreaming and she was remembering. Somewhere below the level of consciousness she was aware of a thin

subvocal whimper throbbing out in a continuous mono-
tone – the voice of all the weak and thin-blooded who
could not face the bright crisp Canadian winter.

But *she* was Genevieve Forquier – born to the clear
icy days, the sub-zero nights, the exhilaration of
skimming across the thick ice coating of a frozen lake
on shining silver blades while the timid, the shy, the
admiring watched enviously.

Genevieve – swooping in a figure 8, dipping in a
swallow's glide, while a portable phonograph somewhere on the sidelines blared out the enticing rhythm
of 'The Skater's Waltz'. Genevieve Forquier – not
quite Olympic status – not quite yet. But definitely
Olympic material. Oh, shades of Walter Mitty! The
next Olympics – or the next – and just watch Genevieve!

Grimly, relentlessly, she closed her ears to everything but 'The Skater's Waltz', ignoring the rising
whimper in the background, the strange emptiness of
the frozen lake, the eerie silence, devoid of laugh or
murmur, surrounding her. Oh, especially she closed
her ears to that constant, irritating endless whine!

She was Genevieve Forquier again. Stubbornly she
clung to the moment, the dream, the memory. Genevieve – gliding across a frozen lake in Quebec.

Over there on the lakeside, by the blazing bonfire,
Paul Jarvis waited for her to come in off the ice, to
return to a level where he could meet her as an equal.
Paul Jarvis, newly arrived from the Old World to seek
his fortune in the New. Paul Jarvis who could, at this
moment, offer her little except a cup of hot chocolate
topped by a marshmallow and an arm around her
shoulders to further warm her. And yet, it was enough.

Da-da-de-dum, Dum-dum-de-dee . . . Slightly tinny, slightly scratched, the record poured its melody across the lake. It was one of those glorious cold sunny days, with the world locked in the heart of an endless January – before any hint of thaw profaned the arctic air.

'*With a crystalline delight* . . .'

The poem always returned to Genevieve at moments like this. On the shore, every twig on every tree was encased in a thin sparkling ice that brought meaning to the poetry. The bright cold sunlight struck silver-gilt-diamond reflections off the coating ice and turned the world into a crystal scene: endlessly bright, artificial and uncaring. Preserved for all time in the deep ice-bound heart of January.

Dum-dum-de-da . . . Faster and faster spun Gene-vieve Forquier. Towards dizziness, towards Fate, towards the future that awaited her, shivering patiently in the unnatural temperature of a strange country, waiting for the warmth of a smile, a friendship, a love.

Da-da-de-dum . . . She swerved away from the shore again, although she was shivering herself now. Still clinging to the dream, as though the shivering had presaged what awakening must bring, she tried to prolong the dream, the memory. But the chill struck through to the marrow of her bones now. For the sake of her health, her sanity, she must relinquish the dream soon – or be lost for ever.

'*Mummy* . . . MUMMY . . .' The scream cut through her, pulling her upright in the strange bed, the remnants of the dream – and the evanescent joy it had brought – falling away from her.

'MUMMY!' She was fully awake now and reaching

for her robe, her child's voice reverberating in her ears.

'I'm coming, darling,' she called. 'Mummy's coming, Alexandra.'

The dream not quite shaken off, stumbling in a room strangely unfamiliar to her, she fought her way to the doorway and down the hallway to her daughter's room.

'Mummy, Mummy – it *hurts*!' Sandy was doubled up beneath the covers. '*Mum*-MEE!' The voice rose in a shriek of anguish.

'All right, darling, all right. Mummy's here.' A stupid thing to say. What good could merely being Mummy and being here do in a situation like this?

She found the light switch, snapped it on. 'What's the matter, darling?'

'It *hurts*!' Sandy twisted in pain, clutching her stomach.

Mrs Paul Jarvis, softened by too many years of soft living and, latterly, weakened by her own domestic problems, might have been unequal to the problem.

Fortunately, thanks to recent events – and the dream – the young Genevieve Forquier was in the ascendant. Genevieve, who had worked as a student nurse in a Quebec City hospital.

'*Mon Dieu*! Appendicitis!' Even as she made the diagnosis, every fibre of her being rejected it – and yet knew that it was true. Here, in this strange unfriendly country, this bleak dank climate, with no one to turn to, in a house miles from the nearest hospital, the nearest help – her only child had been stricken by appendicitis. She had awakened from a dream to face a nightmare.

'Mummy . . .' Sandy had subsided into whimpering pain. 'Mummy, my stomach hurts. It hurts so much . . .'

Make it better, the unspoken plea. But this was more than a skinned knee or a cut finger. You couldn't kiss this and make it better.

'I know, darling, I know.' She looked down at Sandy's flushed, contorted face and brushed a hand lightly over the burning forehead. 'I'll call the doctor. He'll be here soon.'

Even as she spoke, she was pulling the extension phone towards her and opening the drawer of the bedside table to find the little pad with the emergency phone numbers jotted down. In the beginning, Paul had laughed at her habit of keeping a set of emergency phone numbers by every telephone extension. He had thought one set of numbers in a central location was enough, whereas she had maintained that, in an emergency, you might not want – or be able – to leave the nearest telephone in order to hunt for a pad of paper located in some other place. For an instant, she felt a flash of triumph at her foresight, then remembered. There was no Paul at hand to say *I told you so* to. She faced her emergencies alone these days – and had done so for quite a long time now.

The burring ring at the other end of the line stopped abruptly and she heard the doctor's voice, still blurred with sleep. 'Who's there? What is it?'

'Genevieve Jarvis,' she answered quickly, pulling her thoughts together, fearful he might think it a hoax call and ring off. 'I'm sorry to disturb you, doctor, but it's an emergency. My little girl, Sandy – Alexandra. I'm afraid it's appendicitis. I think you'd better send an ambulance.'

'Ambulance?' He was alert now. 'Mrs Jarvis . . .

Jarvis . . .' He seemed to be flipping through some mental files. 'You're quite a way out, aren't you? Well beyond town . . .'

'Dower House Cottage,' she reminded him crisply. 'About fifteen miles along the main road and then you take the left fork just before the road turns towards the motorway.'

Sandy whimpered abruptly and part of Genevieve's careful control slipped. 'Please hurry,' she begged.

'Hurry?' There was an uneasy note in his voice. 'Mrs Jarvis, have you looked out of the window?'

'No.' Automatically, she did so. A white mist was rolling across the lawn, growing thicker as she watched. 'It's . . .' She paused to steady her voice. 'It seems to be getting foggy.'

'It may be *getting* foggy up there, but we have a solid blanket of it down here in the valley. We can't see two feet ahead of us. There'll be no hurrying done tonight – this morning.'

'Oh, but – '

'We'll be as fast as we can,' he assured her. 'I'm just pointing out that we won't be able to get up any speed. What's the little girl's temperature?'

'I don't know. I haven't – ' She pushed the memory away. The thermometer was in the medicine cabinet at Dower House. But she could not mention that, go into explanations. 'I haven't a thermometer here. It must be over a hundred. Oh, please, hurry!'

'I'll send out the ambulance,' he said. 'It can start while I'm getting dressed. One or the other of us ought to get through. If it gets there first, don't wait for me. If I don't find you there, I'll make my way to the hospital. Meanwhile, the child can be receiving professional attention. One of us ought to be there in an hour or so.'

'An hour!' She was aghast. 'But – '

'Perhaps longer. You haven't seen one of our pea-soupers before, have you, Mrs Jarvis?'

'No.' Dimly, she remembered a press picture in a Quebec newspaper once of a London double-decker bus being preceded by a conductor carrying a lantern, both proceeding at walking pace.

'You've *got* to hurry,' she pleaded, as though her urgency might cut through the fog. 'Sandy's in *such* pain. She may not be able to last another hour – '

The grim arithmetic added up in her mind: an hour, perhaps two hours, for the ambulance to reach Dower House Cottage; plus an additional hour, perhaps two finding its way back to the hospital. And Sandy? What of Sandy in all that time?

'It might rupture . . .' she whispered. 'Peritonitis . . . She's so small . . . she's only eight years old . . .'

'We'll get there as soon as we can,' the doctor said wearily, sympathy underlining the exasperation in his voice. An hysterical mother would not improve the situation one bit.

'I know,' she said. 'I know, but – ' The endless, hopeless, perennial question she had heard so many other laymen asking: 'Isn't there anything I can do to help?'

'Keep her warm, keep her comfortable . . .' The placebos rolled out mechanically. 'Try to relax yourself. It won't help if you get into a state. We'll be there as soon as we can.'

'Yes. Thank you. Do you think – ?' But he had rung

off. Not surprisingly. He had to get dressed, notify the ambulance and hospital, and then face hours of driving through a thick fog. There was no time to indulge in metaphorical hand-holding over the telephone.

'Mummy...' A quiet whimper now. Was the face a little less flushed, the small fists a trifle less tightly clenched? Could Sandy hold out for the hours necessary to transport her to the hospital?

And wasn't there *anything* she could do? Frantically, Genevieve cast her mind back to those years – those few years – barely more than two, when she had walked shining hospital corridors, training to be a nurse. But that had been so long ago and medicine had changed so much since then. She should have finished her nursing course and qualified before allowing Paul Jarvis to draw her into his own life. She should at least have taken First Aid courses periodically to keep herself up to date with the newest methods.

But it was too late to agonize over what she should have done. She had not. And now it was her own child who might have to pay for her carelessness.

Outside, the fog had risen from the ground nearly waist-high and wisps were trailing across the lawn at a higher level, blurring the outlines of Dower House itself. There was a light shining in the upper bedroom window, so someone was up – or at least, awake – over there. It did not make her feel any the less isolated.

'Mummy . . .' The exhausted whimper was fainter still. Was Sandy drifting back to sleep as the pain loosened its grip – or was she losing consciousness? Could the attack be over? Or was it a momentary remission, from which the pain would return to tear at the small body more viciously than before?

Genevieve tested Sandy's forehead again. The fever did not seem to have gone down.

Time had stopped. She looked at her watch. Not five minutes had ticked away since she had been speaking to the doctor. He would hardly have left his house yet. Perhaps he was still trying to notify the hospital to dispatch an ambulance. How many ambulances would be at the disposal of such a small hospital? Perhaps there was only one. Perhaps that one was already out on a call, crawling through the blinding fog, lost . . .

In that case, the doctor *must* get through. Although it would not be so comfortable for Sandy to lie on the back seat of whatever car the doctor drove . . .

Paul had a Rolls-Royce in the garage at Dower House. He had driven down in it on Friday with his . . . secretary.

Perhaps they could borrow that if the ambulance didn't arrive. If Paul had been a different sort of man, they could have bundled Sandy into it already and been on their way. But Paul was a week-end resident at his country estate – and not many week-ends, at that. Furthermore, they had usually been business entertaining week-ends – he had not mixed with the locals nor taken time to explore his surroundings. He would not even know where the hospital was located, much less the quickest route to get to it.

And, if *she* had been a different sort of person, she would have finished her studies and been of more use in the present situation. If she had been stronger and more resolute, she would have insisted on a life of her own, rather than allowing her own interests to become absorbed in Paul's so completely. But she had become engulfed in the whirling excitement of Paul's world –

as had so many others. His meteoric rise through the business skies, the ease with which he seemed to form companes, attract capital, exude confidence and success had seduced them all. No, she had not been the only one to sink her interests in his own. It had been more exciting, more comfortable, to be swept up in the train of his comet rather than to continue to follow the cold, lonely, distant and very small star that had once been her own.

'Mummy . . .' Sandy's eyes were open again, frightened and hurt.

'The doctor's on his way.' Genevieve tried to comfort her. 'So is the ambulance. We'll have you in hospital in no time – ' Her voice faltered. 'No time at all.'

'But it hurts *now*.' The sad, patient little voice tried to explain. 'It hurts awfully.'

'Then we'll try to help now.' Genevieve tried to sound confident.

Keep her warm, keep her comfortable, the doctor had said. Another moan from Sandy sent Genevieve rushing desperately towards the kitchen. A hot-water bottle. It was not much – but it might be some help in keeping the appendix under control until the ambulance arrived.

Oh, if only she had kept on with her nursing.

But it was too late for regrets. Genevieve snapped on the switch at the door and light flooded the kitchen and battled its way through the rising mist to shed a faint radiance into the night.

CHAPTER III

Even now, crouched in the bushes, miles away, he could hardly believe that he had succeeded. His ears still strained for the sounds of pursuit, his eyes squinted against the roiling grey fog to discern the darker shapes of retribution. Trying to control the rasp of his lungs as they gulped down the soft dampness, he shrank closer to the earth, trying not to move a muscle – a fox gone to ground, frozen into immobility the better to evade the hunt.

But no one was hunting for him – that was the beauty of it. So beautiful that he was reluctant to believe it, even as every passing silent moment assured him it was true. He had done it. Against odds so insupportable that few had ever achieved it before. And most of them had had help – either inside or outside, or both.

But he had done it alone. And successfully. He had escaped from Dartmoor Prison.

Despite the chill of the cold night fog, a faint glow of warmth burned steadily deep inside him. They'd said it couldn't be done. But he had shown them. And he'd show them a lot more before he was done.

Forethought, that was what it had taken. He clutched the polythene-wrapped packet he had so recently dug up from its hiding place on the moor. Forethought. Even though he'd never believed that he might be caught and sentenced, he'd still had the forethought to collect half a dozen guns and supplies of ammunition, and wrap each parcel in polythene and bury them in widely scattered, but easily marked, positions around the moor. In case.

And the knives, too – ah yes, the knives. Although he'd hated to bury the pretty shining things, he was glad now that he had included one in each parcel.

Even if he hadn't needed one of those parcels in the future, they would not have been a loss but an investment. He could still sell the others – or the knowledge of their whereabouts. There were plenty of men in Dartmoor who weren't planning to stay there for an instant longer than necessary, and who would pay well for the knowledge that would let them pick up an extra passport on their way to freedom.

Whether they ever got the chance to use it, or not.

The beauty of it was that there were still five guns and knives buried out there on the moor, five potential sources of future income. Meanwhile, the one in his hand proved the value of his forethought.

Forethought and opportunism, that was what had helped him to escape and now pointed the way to freedom. He'd seen the sudden opportunity to escape and taken advantage of it, even knowing how high the odds must be against such a chance paying off. And yet, it had.

So far, so good. What he needed now was food, a change of clothing, and a way to get out of the country. From here, that meant he must head for the coast and look for someone with a small boat. A small boat and an even smaller amount of courage when faced by a desperate man with a gun.

Where was he, right now, in relation to the coast? Which way should he be heading?

The fog was thick and dank. Frustrating when the moon was still clear overhead. It was strange, uncanny almost, to be able to see the moon and stars so distinctly when, close to earth, it was impossible to distinguish the landscape a few yards ahead.

He hadn't counted on the fog. It might work for him, or it might work against him. At the moment, it was neutral, or perhaps even against him. Since it was unlikely that his escape would be discovered before morning, the fog could not hamper his pursuers, but it might hamper him.

He was breathing more easily now. Not relaxed – he would never relax until he heard the din of a foreign language beating against his ears, felt his eyes seared by the brightness of a sun unshadowed by English clouds – or fog. But he was beginning to believe in the escape he had accomplished, beginning to feel that he could go on and accomplish the rest of it. To be free, and to reach a point far beyond the possibility of pursuit. A country where they had no extradition treaty with England, no matter what the crime.

Abruptly, the fog swirled heavily around him, enveloping him in a deep pocket so dark and thick that it seemed to blot out even his thought processes. He coughed, muffled the cough, and coughed again, as the wet acrid mist clawed at his throat. Then he shivered.

It was cold. Bloody cold. He needed an overcoat. And a good stiff drink. How long had it been? No point in thinking about that. He shivered again. Concentrate on the present. The next step – and the next. Another shiver.

So, first warmth. Then food, drink, clothing, and the coast – not necessarily in that order, but in fairly rapid succession, whatever order. But where? And when? How soon?

A bright arrow shot through the thick white mist. Somewhere above and ahead, a light had gone on in some house.

A house. Nearby. He raised his head, blinking against the faint radiance, following it to its source. A big house. The light was coming from an upstairs window – a long luxurious window, which bespoke floors beneath it and floors above it. A big, wealthy house.

There were other people awake, unknowingly sharing this bleak dank night with him. Strong, rich, powerful people, secure and warm within the sheltering walls of a great house while he shivered in the fog outside.

Mesmerized by the warm bright beam, he began unconsciously creeping closer to it.

Another searchlight pierced the fog abruptly. He shrank back, momentarily panicked.

No, not a searchlight. They weren't after him – yet. Besides, he was too far away from the searchlights to see them, too far from the sirens to hear the alarm. He was far away from them all. A safe distance? A distance, anyway.

The light was just a light. Another lamp switched on in another room by another insomniac. It had nothing to do with him. Other people were living their own lives, unaware of his existence. As yet.

This light was lower than the other. A smaller, more humble house.

The high beam and the low beam shone out into the fog, crossing but not quite meeting. Beneath them, they illuminated a restless white mist which was crawling across the wide smooth lawn that separated them. There was plenty of space, but no fence or hedge between the houses. Did that mean they were part of the same estate? The Manor House and the servants' cottage, perhaps?

He began moving forward again. Houses meant warmth, food, clothing. Which one would be the best choice?

A second light went on in the cottage. That meant people restless, moving around, apt to investigate strange noises in another part of the house and bump into an intruder. He wasn't ready for any confrontations – not yet. *He* would decide the time and place for challenges.

So, the big house looked more attractive for his purposes. A quiet man could slip in and out unnoticed in a house with that many rooms. In all that space, you had room to manoeuvre, to keep a few steps ahead of anyone who might choose to investigate strange noises – providing any noise carried to an occupied room from the lower regions. The light was in an upstairs bedroom, someone who'd got up to go to the bathroom, perhaps. Or, unable to sleep, had settled down with a book to read for a while. There was every good chance that they would stay on the upper storey and not discover there had been an intruder downstairs until morning.

It was possible that there were servants asleep in the lower regions, but in old-fashioned houses like this they tended to have servants' quarters on the top floor. It was even more possible that the servants didn't live in at all – that they lived in the small cottage where someone was moving about so restlessly.

But it was certain that there was a kitchen in the big house. On the ground floor, or possibly in the basement. A kitchen, with plenty of food and warmth. He could refuel there and then choose his moment to venture into the upper regions in search of a change of clothing.

The light drew him like a beacon. A slightly darker shadow among the swirling shadows of the fog, he advanced on Dower House.

CHAPTER IV

'*Mummee – Mummee –* '

The hot-water bottle slipped from Genevieve's fingers and flopped limply into the sink. Was there a new note of urgency in Sandy's cry? Was the appendix rupturing even now?

'I'm coming, darling.' She retrieved the hot-water bottle and forced herself to fill it, although her shaking hands threatened to spoil her perilous aim and send the scalding water cascading over the hot-water bottle rather than into it. At least she should be grateful that there *was* a hot-water bottle in the inventory of Dower House Cottage.

'Here we are.' She tried to keep her voice cheerful and confident as she smiled down at Sandy. 'Now, we'll just tuck this in on top of your naughty tummy – '

'No!' Sandy pushed it away. 'No! It's too hot. It's boiling!'

'It *has* to be hot, darling. That's the whole idea.' She captured Sandy's protesting hand, tucked the hot-water bottle in and secured it with the blanket. 'Just take it easy, darling.' She stroked the feverish forehead. 'Relax. Get used to it. It's there to help you.'

'NO-o-o,' Sandy whimpered. 'No-o-o-o.' But the physical act of pushing the hot-water bottle away again was obviously too much for her. She tossed her protesting head back and forth on the pillow. 'No-o-o.'

'It will help you,' Genevieve murmured softly, hypnotically. 'Nice, warm, *friendly* hot-water bottle. It's there to help you, darling.'

The damp flushed forehead seemed to grow hotter. Was it safe to give her another aspirin, perhaps two? It might bring down the fever – but would it attack the basic cause?

Genevieve glanced frantically towards the window. She could deceive herself no longer. The fog was growing worse by the moment. There could be little hope that the ambulance would quickly find its way through the obscured maze of country lanes to Dower House Cottage – and even less hope that it might ever manage to crawl back safely to the county hospital with its precious cargo.

'Mummee –' The voice rose in an hysterical wail, not really expecting Mummy to be able to do anything about the nightmare they were both enmeshed in, but unable to visualize a stronger, higher authority to which to turn. 'Mummee – it hurts. It hurts so much!'

'Yes, darling. Yes, I know.' Genevieve, bitterly conscious of her helplessness, went through all the useless, meaningless gestures once again: smoothing the pillow, straightening the blankets, stroking the brow, making all the soothing, useless sounds. 'It's all right, darling. It's going to be all right.' And knowing, all the while, that nothing might ever be all right again.

Spontaneous remission. The phrase came back to her from her early nursing days. The cold medical explanation for the 'miracles' claimed by the fervid, the impressionable, the religious fanatics who were certain that a visit to Ste Anne de Beaupré – crawling up the endless steps on their knees – had accomplished what medical science had not had in its power. Spontaneous remission. Why couldn't it happen now?

Sandy sighed, and slept. Or had she just lost consciousness? In any case, her eyes were closed, her breathing regular, and she ceased to struggle against the hot-water bottle pressed against her side. How long would this respite last?

Trembling, Genevieve moved away from the bed, not quite daring to believe in a fortune good enough to allow this nightmare to pass away entirely. Then she turned back and stretched out a trembling hand to rest against her daughter's forehead – still hot, so very hot.

How hot? She withdrew her hand. Somewhere there was a thermometer that would tell her. Somewhere – but not here.

The thermometer was in Dower House itself. The one place she could not go. Not now. Not with Paul in residence – with *her.*

And so, here they were. Paul's legal wife. Paul's child. Outcasts in Dower House Cottage. The disowned. The disinherited. Off with the old, on with the new!

Genevieve drew a deep quivering breath, pulling herself back from the verge of hysteria. This could do no good. She forced herself to move away again, to

walk out into the kitchen, to refill the kettle and set it on
the hob. A cup of coffee. That was not the answer —
but it would help. Help her through the dark and
frightening hours that stretched before her. Until the
ambulance came. Surely, the ambulance *must* come.
The alternative was unthinkable.

She let the motor mechanisms for small simple tasks
take over, lulling herself into a momentary sense of
security. She opened the cupboard and took out a cup
and saucer. She found the jar of instant coffee—*no! Don't
think about the Costa Rican blend, the percolator, the
porcelain coffee set — all, all in Dower House.* They
belonged to another lifetime. They were a world away.

She must concentrate on the here and now — no
matter how unsatisfactory, how perilous, it might be.
This was all she had left. This tiny kitchen in a servants'
cottage. And Sandy.

All that was left out of the hopeful joyous years,
when she and Paul had both been young, totally
involved with each other, building for a future they had
never dreamed might devolve into anything like this.

The kettle shrilled abruptly, emitting a jet of steam.
She turned off the gas and poured the water into the
waiting cup. Before she could add milk, Sandy cried
out again. Genevieve abandoned the coffee and hurried
upstairs.

Sandy was sobbing quietly now. She had pushed the
hot-water bottle out of the bed and it lay on the floor.
Perhaps it wouldn't have been of much use anyway.

'The doctor's coming,' Genevieve soothed frantically.
'He'll be here soon.' How soon? How long could Sandy
go on bearing such pain? How long could she bear to

listen to her daughter's agony?

'Don't want the doctor,' Sandy moaned fretfully. 'I want – I want my Daddy!'

Well, why not? Paul *was* her father, and he *was* within calling distance. Why should he be allowed to opt out of all his responsibilities? What had happened between them should not rebound on poor, innocent Sandy. Let Paul come and behave like a father, even though he was no longer interested in behaving like a husband.

'All right, darling.' Genevieve straightened her shoulders and reached for the telephone. She did not need to look up *this* number.

'All right. Daddy's coming.'

CHAPTER V

He thought it was Harlow again when the telephone rang so soon after he had walked away from it. He wheeled and went back to it, snatching it up, snapping, 'Yes, what is it?' without bothering to disguise the impatience in his voice. Harlow might have turned up another bit of genuinely important information, or he might simply have thought up another smirking innuendo he wished to deliver. Whichever it was, Harlow reacted best to a touch of the whip.

'Paul?' The voice at the other end of the line was not Harlow's. He felt the accustomed sinking feeling of guilt as he recognized the familiar voice.

'Genevieve – ' He lowered his own voice, conscious that Lillian had stopped packing and was standing there listening.

'What is it?' Paul glanced incredulously at his watch, unable to believe that she could be awake and telephoning him at this hour. 'Is anything wrong?'

'Yes, there is.' The quick defensiveness in her voice snapped at him. *Would I be calling you at all if there wasn't?* Genevieve had her pride. Too much pride perhaps, but that was Genevieve.

'Paul . . . it's Sandy.'

He had known she was going to say that. It was the only reason she would forget her pride – humble herself, as she saw it, to call him.

'Paul . . . she's sick. Very sick. I – I'm frightened – ' Her voice broke. He heard her take a deep breath and catch back a sob before she continued. 'I've spoken to the doctor. He's sending an ambulance. But it may not be able to get through. The fog – '

He cursed briefly and luridly, finding no release in the mechanical words. Lillian was beside him now, listening with him, her golden head pressed against his own as though to drive out memories of the darker head that had once been as closely pressed.

'I – I'm afraid – ' Genevieve's voice caught again. 'It looks like appendicitis – There's nothing I can do for her. She wants – She wants her Daddy – '

'All right,' he said. 'I'm coming.' He did not look at Lillian. He felt her head nodding in agreement against his. But . . . *had* there been a hesitation, as though waiting for his decision before endorsing it?

He replaced the receiver and still did not look at her, feeling numbed by the sudden accumulation of blows from a Fate which he was accustomed to see smiling upon him.

'It will be all right,' Lillian said softly. 'We have the helicopter on the way, remember?'

'Of course.' Strength flowed back into him. Outside the fog blanketed the landscape, hiding the ground in a thick amorphous layer of ectoplasm. Wheeled vehicles could be delayed, tricked into wrong turnings, and hopelessly lost in the deceptive mist. But a helicopter flew above the traitorous earth, immune to the visual distortions at ground level. The helicopter could swoop like a hawk through the layers of obscurity and soar upwards again, carrying them beyond the mist into light and safety.

'I'll telephone ahead,' Lillian offered, 'while you go over there and tell them and help them get ready.' *Them*, not *her*, never *her*. Yet, could Lillian be blamed? His own guilt kept him from thinking in terms of *her* himself.

'The Great Ormond Street Hospital for Sick Children,' Lillian said. 'That will be the best place. They're geared to emergencies and helicopters flying in. We can land in Coram's Fields and the hospital will have an ambulance waiting to whisk Sandy over to the hospital.'

Lillian would know about these things. She had had a small flat in Mecklenburgh Square before it had somehow become simpler for her to move in and share the executive flat in Mayfair.

'It's *so* lucky the helicopter was on its way in any case,' Lillian said. 'It means no time will be lost.'

'Yes,' he agreed, moving towards the door. 'Very lucky.' Lucky, too, that he had allowed a persuasive

salesman to talk him into a Sikorsky 55, large enough
to lift Chairman and Board members to the scene of any
emergency. It meant there would be room to spare for
two more passengers, even though one of them would
be stretched out across a row of seats. In the most
curious ways, it paid off not to stint.

'I'll arrange everything.' Lillian accompanied him
to the front door, once more the efficient executive
secretary.

'I'd appreciate it if you would.' He sounded ridicu-
lously stilted and formal. They both did for two people
who, just a short time ago –

'Oh! The fog *is* thick!' Lillian shivered in the dank
mist as he opened the front door. 'I'd better switch on
the tennis court lights now, or you might get lost just
trying to cross the lawn.' She shivered again, as
though something colder and deeper than the fog were
stretching out chill fingers for her.

'Go inside,' Paul said. 'It won't do anyone any good
if you become ill, too. I'll be back as soon as I can.'

'Will you?' The murmur was so faint that he was
not sure whether he had heard it. She stepped back
into the doorway, still shivering.

'Please do.' Lillian's voice was suddenly as wispy
and evanescent as the mist. 'The moor is different
tonight. I'm not sure I like it any more. I – I don't
want to be alone.'

Neither does Genevieve. He could not voice the
thought. He wished that it had not occurred to him.
The issues were no longer clear. If they both needed
him, where did his duty lie?

With Sandy. For the moment, that was the only
thread of loyalty he must follow through the com-

plicated maze surrounding him. *Sandy*. The most innocent of them all – and the one who might suffer most.

'Go inside,' Paul said again. 'I'll be back.'

CHAPTER VI

Lillian watched until he blurred into the fog, an underwater figure swimming slowly through foam turned opalescent by the floodlights of the tennis court.

At least there was no wind. That was something to be thankful for. She hated being aloft in turbulence.

She heard Paul call out, although she could not distinguish the words, and knew that he had reached Dower House Cottage safely. The fog was evidently muffling sound as well as blurring vision. Suddenly, she did not like Dower House and its surrounding acres as much as she used to. It was a different place on a foggy November night. A place she could lose enthusiasm for very easily.

She looked upwards. Neither sight nor sound of the helicopter yet. How long would it take to get here? Harlow claimed to have already dispatched it before he rang. But Harlow's claims were not always to be trusted. He might have waited to be sure that Dower House answered and that Paul was really there and had not slipped away somewhere else on a business trip. Paul's secret business trips were ever a thorn in Harlow's side. He could not bear the thought that there were fragments of other people's lives that he knew nothing about. Perhaps that was what kept him forever on the alert for every hint of intrigue. It made him a valuable ally against Paul's enemies, but a tiresome colleague when things were quiet and his boredom found an outlet in prying into the affairs of those on his own side. How Harlow had enjoyed it when he discovered the truth about Paul and her.

Lillian shivered again and stepped back inside, shutting the door behind her. She hesitated, then left the light on over the front entrance. In a fog like this, every ray of light would help guide the helicopter in to a landing.

She was chilled to the bone from just that short time of standing in the doorway. She moved towards the kitchen at the rear of the house. She would put the kettle on before she telephoned Harlow and finished packing. She could use a cup of coffee. Paul would want one, too, when he came back.

Automatically, scarcely noticing she was doing so, she snapped on the lights in every room she passed. They never bothered to draw the curtains in the evening. They were not overlooked by Dower House Cottage — and who else was there to see in? Brightness flooded the rooms in the wake of her progress, but seemed to stop at the window panes, as though the fog beyond were too impenetrable even to attempt. Still, each additional tiny glimmer of light might help mark out Dower House from the sky.

She did not admit to herself the thought lurking just beneath her conscious level: if Paul were to look towards the house from the cottage, he would see it glowing through the fog like a great lighthouse, warning him of the shoals, calling him back to warmth and safety. And her.

In the kitchen, she turned all the lights on, even in the pantry, filled the kettle, took two cups and saucers from the cupboard and, after a moment, the vacuum flask as well. It might be wise to fill it with coffee and take it with them. One could never be sure how long the journey back to London would take.

But now she must ring Harlow. It would be easier if he made the arrangements with Great Ormond Street Children's Hospital from the London end. While they were talking, she might even be able to find out exactly when he had dispatched the helicopter and how soon it might reasonably be expected to arrive. Once he recognized a genuine emergency, Harlow could be depended upon to pull out all the stops and get things organized.

She lit the gas and turned it low under the kettle. By the time she finished telephoning, the kettle should be boiling.

She would telephone from upstairs, she decided. That way, she could keep watch from the window, both for the helicopter and for Paul coming back. Looking down on the fog, there might be a better view.

Lillian shivered again. While she was upstairs, she had better change into warmer clothing. It was going to be a long cold night.

CHAPTER VII

He dropped to a crouch, ready to fling himself head-long and flattening out on the ground as the fog brightened suddenly and turned luminescent. He recognized the peculiar brilliance of searchlights and, for a panic-stricken moment, thought he must have doubled back on his tracks in some way, gone in the traditional circle, and come back close to the point of escape. His nerves cringed, waiting for the wailing crescendo of cheated fury that would be the sirens shrieking his escape to the world.

But there was only the muted click of a door opening and the soft murmur of voices. He had approached closer to the big house than he had thought. Lucky he hadn't been trying to get inside right now. A light in an upstairs bedroom was one thing, but who would have thought that ordinary citizens would be up and about at this hour?

And why? He recognized that he was not particularly expert in the ways of ordinary citizens, but he could not believe that they usually went prowling around in the pre-dawn fog. They were normally in bed and asleep – except in an emergency.

Could *he* be the emergency? Was it possible that his escape had been discovered and that the police were telephoning the citizenry in remote outposts to alert them to the fact that a dangerous criminal was on the loose?

But the man and the woman were lingering on the doorstep, talking with some urgency, but without alarm. They had not stared around into the fog, as they would have done if they feared danger might be advancing on them from some unspecified source.

No, when they lifted their heads, they looked in one direction only – towards the smaller house where windows were also alight at this unlikely hour. That seemed to be the cause of their concern.

He straightened cautiously and moved forward, still bending low. If he could get close enough to hear what they were saying, he might be able to guess how many other people were in the house. And what, if any, defences they might have against unwanted callers.

'*I'll be back,*' he heard the man say before moving off in the direction of the small house. The woman remained on the doorstep, the mist turning her hair into a gold halo and blurring the edges of her tightly-cinched turquoise housecoat. Yes, she was probably worth coming back to.

But what could send a man away from her on a night like this? Curious now, he was torn between following the man and staying with the woman.

As he watched, she gave a convulsive shudder and moved back into the house, leaving the light burning over the door. Still hesitating, he saw that she was turning on all the lights as she moved through the house. He could chart her progress from the front door through to the rear of the house, presumably the kitchen.

That told him what he wanted to know. Snapping on every light was the reaction of a woman left alone in a house. Dead giveaway, that was. As though light itself were some sort of protection – which, in the ordinary way, it might be. But tonight was not an ordinary night.

His curiosity aroused now, he turned to follow the man. But, *I'll be back, too*, he promised the lighted house.

The fog muffled footsteps, hiding any sounds of pursuit as he hurried to catch up with the man, but set him to shivering so badly that his teeth began to chatter. He ground them tightly, trying to silence them. Soon, soon, he would allow himself to slide into the warmth and shelter of one of the houses. But first, he had to find out just a bit more about the situation he had stumbled into.

The man halted on the doorstep of the cottage and put his hand into his pocket, automatically, in the gesture of one reaching for his key. Then, after a momentary hesitation, he brought his hand out empty and rang the doorbell instead.

Interesting. Had he forgotten his key? Or was there a reason why he shouldn't use it? Even from this distance, a sense of embarrassment radiated from the figure on the doorstep.

The door opened slowly and a dark-haired woman stood there outlined by the light burning behind her in the hallway. She was wearing a dark red heavy dressing-gown and she, too, radiated embarrassment.

'I . . . I'm glad you've come, Paul.' The voice was so faint the listening man could barely catch the words.

'Of course I've come.' The man's voice was louder, but did not seem any more assured. 'Did you think I wouldn't?'

Greedy. A woman in each house. Two houses. Two women. And how much else besides? While other poor devils had nothing and were alone and cold and shivering out in the bleak wet fog. But not for much longer.

'Paul – ' The woman stepped back to let the man into the house. It was done in slow motion, reluctantly perhaps, but it was done. 'Paul, I'm frightened. She's getting worse. Oh, Paul, I'm so afraid – '

'It will be all right – ' The man stretched out a hand awkwardly, as though he would pat her shoulder, possibly even embrace her. But the woman flinched and he snatched the hand back even more awkwardly.

'The ambulance will never get through in this fog!' the woman cried out, her voice subtly accusing. She frowned over his shoulder, trying to penetrate the solid white mist that blanketed the world. 'Nothing could move through it. And Sandy will – '

'Sandy will be all right.' The man's voice was firm and strong now, as though he had emerged from a morass on to land that he was sure of. 'There's a helicopter on the way. We'll have her out of this and safely in London in a couple of hours – '

The door swung shut behind him, cutting off the remainder of his reassurances. But the listener in the fog had heard enough.

A helicopter. That explained the lights turned on everywhere outside – landing lights to guide the helicopter down through the fog. And up again. Up – to freedom.

London be damned! A helicopter could lift him across the Channel. Better – much better – than a boat. And faster.

His luck was in. He wasn't shivering any longer. The glow of satisfaction warmed him physically as well as mentally. He'd be out of this in no time, safe from pursuit, ready to take up the new life he'd been planning for so long. As soon as the helicopter arrived.

But he had to be ready for it. Ready and waiting. That meant back at the big house. Back where all the lights were blazing out their signal. That was where the helicopter would be landing. And, perhaps, before it landed he might be able to get some food.

He turned his back on Dower House Cottage —
there was nothing there of interest to him — and
started back for the big house.

CHAPTER VIII

'A helicopter?' Genevieve stepped back slowly, allowing him into the hallway and closed the door behind
him, her face alight with hope. It seemed that he had
done something right, for a change. 'So quickly?'

'It was on the way when you called.' He disdained
to take the easy way out, to let her feel gratitude for
something that had not been of his doing. 'I have an
important business meeting in London first thing in
the morning. We can drop you and Sandy off at the
hospital on the way.'

'Of course.' She lowered her eyes. 'Always the
important business meeting. Nothing changes, Paul.'

Quite a few things had changed, were in the process
of changing, which was why she was here now. But it
was not the time to argue that — or to remind her that, if
things had not changed, she and Sandy would be safe
in Montreal right now, Sandy already in a hospital and
receiving expert medical attention. Perhaps she did not
need reminding. The thought could not be very far
from her consciousness at a time like this.

'How *is* Sandy?' he asked.

'Come and see for yourself.' Genevieve led the way
upstairs. 'She's been calling for you. She might be
better — now that you are here.'

Was there a subtle accusation in that remark? Because he wasn't 'here' all the time? Or was it because of his feeling of guilt that he was reading hidden meanings into every remark? That had been the start of it perhaps, back when he was first becoming aware of Lillian and feared that Genevieve had begun to suspect. But how long must the feeling continue? Now that the whole situation was in the process of being sorted out, surely these guilt feelings ought to abate and allow him to live in peace.

'Daddy!' Sandy's eyelids fluttered upwards and she smiled and turned towards him, trying to sit up. Almost immediately, the pain caught at her and her face twisted. She fell back against the pillows, whimpering.

'Hello, sweetheart. Now, what's the matter with you?' He forced heartiness into his voice, although something inside him had caught and twisted with the small face as though her pain were his own.

'I don't know,' Sandy whispered. 'But it hurts. Oh, Daddy, it hurts awfully!'

'Well, now – ' He knelt by the bed and took one small hand in his. It was hot and damp and clung to him tightly. 'We'll have to do something about that, won't we?'

'Yes . . .' Her eyes were so trusting. She was too young to be aware of his utter helplessness in such a situation. For her, Daddy could still fix everything.

'I think we'll take you back to London,' he said reassuringly. 'You'll be more comfortable there in a nice hospital with lots of nice doctors and nurses around you who know what they're doing and can help you.'

He looked up and unexpectedly saw the pain in Genevieve's eyes. It had not occurred to him that she could have anything to feel guilty about. He remembered now that she had been in nurse's training when they met. She had given up her training – without, let's be honest, putting up any great fight – when they married and he had wanted his wife to be able to travel around with him and act as his hostess at business dinners. Now their child was ill and she was blaming herself because she could not cope adequately with the emergency.

'This is a job for the experts,' he said, trying to absolve her. Even if she had finished her training and become a Registered Nurse, there was nothing more she could do. This was something for a surgeon to cope with. Surely she was not torturing herself with the delusion that she might have gone on for further training after that, become a doctor, perhaps even a surgeon herself? But guilt recognized no boundaries of absurdity – as he well knew.

Genevieve caught her breath. He *did* believe it was appendicitis, then. It had been her own diagnosis, one which she had conveyed to him over the telephone, but it was frightening to have it confirmed – even by another layman.

'What do you think?' Paul jiggled Sandy's hand coaxingly. 'You're going to have a ride in a helicopter.'

'When?' It brought a flicker of reaction, a faint lightening of the pain in her face as the novelty of the idea momentarily distracted her.

'Any minute now. It's on the way. Soon you'll be able to hear it coming closer and closer . . .' Her eyes had begun to close as, exhausted by the battle with

pain, she began to drift off into . . . sleep? . . . unconsciousness? He lowered his voice to a soothing
drone.

'And it will land on the tennis court – isn't it a good
thing we took the net down?' The small joke brought
no reaction. Her grip on his hand had loosened. She
was breathing lightly but evenly. They were all having
a short respite from her pain.

'When did it start? How long has she been like
this?' Gently disengaging the child's hand, he stood up
and faced Genevieve. With a problem like this between them, he found that he could meet her eyes
again.

'Half an hour? Three-quarters of an hour?' She
shook her head in impatience that she could not even
answer this simple question. 'I – I was asleep. I woke
when she called me. I didn't think to look at a clock
immediately. What difference would it have made? It
happened so suddenly – '

'All right.' He found himself adopting the same
soothing heartiness he had used with Sandy. 'It
doesn't matter. Perhaps she'll be better when she
wakes. These things often come and go. It might be a
false alarm – '

'Even if she *is* better, she may not *stay* better,'
Genevieve interrupted in alarm. 'You won't leave us
here alone?'

'Of course not!' It came out more sharply than he
had intended. He saw Genevieve flush and knew that
his own face was a dull red.

They were words that had never been exchanged
between them in all the past years. Now spoken, even
in this context, they still held meanings it was better

not to examine too closely.

'The helicopter,' Genevieve said swiftly. 'Will it be able to land in this fog?'

'We've put the outside floodlights on,' he said. 'There shouldn't be any difficulty.'

'*Oui*,' Genevieve said. Or had she thoughtfully echoed '*We*'? An acknowledgement – perhaps a reminder – that 'we' had a different meaning these days. '*We*' was no longer Paul-and-Genevieve; '*we*' was now Paul-and-Lillian.

It was no one's fault, but that was the way it was now.

'We've got one of the best pilots available,' Paul said, turning '*we*' into yet another possessive: the Company. 'EngAm spared no expense to acquire him. He can set a helicopter down on an oil rig in the North Sea or on a pocket handkerchief on the side of a mountain. A nice big double tennis court like the one out there will be a holiday for him – fog or not.'

Genevieve smiled faintly in recognition of his efforts to improve her morale. The smile did not reach her eyes, but it was not otherwise a bad effort.

'I'll ring . . . the house,' Paul said. 'Perhaps there'll be some word of how soon we can expect the helicopter. Meanwhile, can you get Sandy dressed?'

'Now?' Genevieve looked at the sleeping child. It would mean awakening her. 'It is better for her to sleep – '

'We'll give her as long as we can.' Once again, the all-purpose '*we*' shifted meaning. It was Paul-and-Genevieve – as it had been in the beginning. He shook his head, trying to clear it. 'That's why I want the estimated time of arrival – '

But the line was busy. Lillian must still be talking to London, either trying to explain the sudden emergency to Harlow, or perhaps talking to the Great Ormond Street Hospital herself, trying to arrange things. He could not get through.

After the third attempt, his nerves were jangling. He could not stay here under Genevieve's watchful eyes any longer. He replaced the receiver with muted violence.

'It's no use,' he said. 'I'll have to get back and find out what's happening. There might be some sudden snag – '

'Oh no!' Genevieve took a step forward in alarm.

'Probably there isn't,' he said. 'Take it easy. If Sandy wakes – or even if she doesn't – try to get her dressed. It's cold out tonight. If you can't, wrap her up warmly – '

'You – ' Genevieve stretched out her hands imploringly – 'You *must* go?' It was not that her pride had crumbled, it was that – where her ailing child was concerned – Genevieve had no pride at all.

'I'm sorry. The London line may be busy – or something may have gone wrong with the wire. It does sometimes in the fog, you know. I've got to find out.' Neither of them could afford pride. If anything happened to Sandy, all the years in between would have no meaning at all.

'I'll be back,' he promised, for the second time that night.

CHAPTER IX

It took a conscious effort on Lillian's part to unclench her teeth and try to speak easily. Harlow had always had that effect on her and, since the personal relationships in Head Office had shifted, it was more pronounced than ever. She would not give him the satisfaction of realizing it.

'Quite a little *family* party you're having down there.' Harlow could not resist the jibe before adding, 'I'll get on to Great Ormond Street and arrange everything at this end.'

'That's good of you,' Lillian said evenly.

'Yes.' Harlow did not dispute that fact. It was above and beyond the call of his ordinary duty – but so was everything he had been doing tonight.

'It won't delay you, will it?' Harlow was struck by a newer, more worrying thought. 'We have quite a bit to get through before the meeting. You'll just drop the child and come straight on here? You won't waste time going to the hospital with her, or anything like that – ?'

Any stupid sentimentality like that, he meant.

'Her mother will stay with her,' Lillian said. 'We'll come straight on to the office.'

'Aaah.' That had answered more than Harlow had dared to ask. She was annoyed with herself for having given more than the barest minimum of information, but she had not wanted Paul to sound unfeeling. Not that a bloodless little stick like Harlow would know the difference.

'That's all right then,' Harlow said cheerfully. 'I'll need at least an hour to brief him on the – '

Lillian stopped listening, her attention diverted by a sound from downstairs. Had Paul returned so soon? She would have called out, but Harlow would have been able to hear her and she would not give him that much satisfaction.

'Yes,' she agreed absently to the question-mark in Harlow's voice, although she had missed the question. She kept her eyes on the door, waiting for Paul to appear. There was silence downstairs now. Could she have been mistaken?

'Good, good,' Harlow said. 'The helicopter should be with you in half an hour or less. If you can all be ready to board, he can take off again immediately. About an hour to return to London, say. Perhaps another ten minutes to offload the child at Coram's Fields, then straight on here. I'll have everything organized at this end.'

There had been no further sound downstairs. Perhaps it was just the creaking of the house she had heard. It was an old house and a large house. There were several things about it she planned to change as soon as it was practicable. Meanwhile, Harlow was waiting for some sort of answer.

'It might take a bit longer than that,' she said. 'The fog is very thick down here – practically solid. You ought to allow an extra half-hour or so to take that into account. The pilot might have difficulty – '

'Nonsense, he'll be flying above the fog. That's the whole point of having a helicopter.' Harlow sounded ruffled, he hated any suggestion that plans he made might go awry, nor did he intend to allow for im-

ponderables. 'Carson is an excellent pilot. He'll have
no trouble with a bit of fog.'

'If you say so.' There was no point in arguing with
Harlow. He had probably never been out of the City
in his life – one couldn't imagine him going off on
holiday like lesser mortals. He had no idea what fog
could be like down here between deep country and the
deeper sea.

'I'll expect you, then.' Abruptly, Harlow rang off,
emphasizing that he had more important things to do
than spend his time gossiping with his employer's
secretary. Or perhaps that was unfair to Harlow. The
news that Paul's wife and child were here at Dower
House (he wasn't to know they were staying in the
Cottage) had shaken him. Just as he thought he had
sorted out the relationships involved, the ground had
shifted under his feet again. Harlow was hopelessly old-
fashioned. To him, Genevieve's presence indicated a
reconciliation; it might be some time before the thought
occurred to him that it could be the prelude to a very
civilized divorce. Meanwhile, he needed time to think
over the implications of what he had just learned.

Lillian found herself reluctant to replace the receiver,
as though she would be releasing her hold on some life-
line if she did so. The vaguely comforting buzzing
reassured her that there was a world out there beyond
the fog, but blunted her hearing to any sound within
the house. Realizing this, she held the receiver away
from her ear, but still did not put it down. Telling
herself it was silly to be so nervous, she listened
intently.

The house was too big, that was part of the trouble.
Perhaps Paul could be persuaded to dispose of it and

buy another house. This was, after all, the property he
had bought for Genevieve in the early days of their
marriage and his first successes. The whole house
shrieked of Genevieve – it had been furnished and
decorated to her taste, with Paul's approval. Or had
Paul paid any real attention at all?

Surely only a Canadian could consider 'The Death of
Montcalm' – however good a copy – a suitable painting
for a family reception room. The 'View of the Plains of
Abraham' in the dining-room was an improvement, but
still uncompromisingly Canadian – and, thus, a
constant reminder of Genevieve.

'The Death of Montcalm' would really be more
suitable for the Boardroom in the City – especially
after this forthcoming Extraordinary General Meeting.
It might serve as a none-too-subtle reminder to certain
members of the Board that Paul Jarvis was a more
powerful figure to oppose than they had thought. If
certain members were still on the Board after today.
EngAm had grown too big, too successful, and eyes
which had once viewed it with pride now watched it
with envy; hands once outstretched to help build now
snatched at it greedily.

And perhaps the 'View of the Plains of Abraham'
could be offered to Genevieve. Better still, perhaps the
whole Dower House estate could be made over to
Genevieve, either in her own name or in trust for
Sandy. Such an action would help assuage Paul's
feeling of guilt, as well as being part of the eventual
property settlement.

Most satisfactorily, that would also leave the way
clear for the purchase of a new country home – a
smaller, friendlier place, and one that would carry

memories of no previous châtelaine.

IF . . . everything went well. If the helicopter pilot were able to find Dower House, could he descend and take off again safely through this fog and whisk them back to London in time for Paul to take over and control the Extraordinary General Meeting that had been called to oust him?

If not, would Paul still have a business empire able to provide such luxuries as country houses?

It was all very well for Harlow, from his ivory tower at the top of the EngAm building in the City to dismiss the fog as a matter of no importance. But, if fog were so negligible, why did Heathrow Airport sometimes close down because of it and divert incoming flights to other airports around the country?

That was the question she should have asked Harlow when she had him on the phone. Why did one always think of the proper rejoinder too late? The dial tone hummed mockingly and she abruptly became aware that she was still holding the receiver, while lost in her thoughts.

Paul might be trying to get through!

She dropped the receiver back on its cradle, where, infuriatingly, it gave a throat-clearing little chirrup, not quite a ring, possibly the tail-end of one.

She snatched it up again, but there was nothing but the dial tone. She replaced the receiver and stood over it, waiting. Silence.

She waited another moment, then remembered that the gas was lit and the kettle must be boiling by this time. If the phone rang, she could take it on the extension downstairs and, meanwhile, she could get on with filling the Thermos and perhaps make a few sandwiches.

She stepped over to the window and looked down. There was no sign of Paul, although he would have to be very close to the house before she could see him. The world was a blurred shapeless mass, no landmark distinguishable. All Harlow's reassurances became as insubstantial as the mist.

Would the helicopter be able to land in this? But they had no real choice; they had to behave as though they believed it could.

With a faint sigh she was not aware she had uttered, Lillian turned away from the window and started downstairs.

CHAPTER X

As he slipped into the front hall, he was momentarily careless. After the muffling silence of the fog, the click of the door latch and the sound of his footsteps on the parquet flooring came as a shock. It was as though gravity had reasserted itself after a temporary period of weightlessness.

More cautiously now, he shifted to tiptoe and moved silently across the hall, blinking in the bright light. Instinctively, he looked for shadows to shelter him, but there were none. He stood revealed should anyone appear at the top of the stairs.

He heard the murmur of voices upstairs. Or was it just one voice speaking in a conversational tone? On the telephone, perhaps. Had he been mistaken in assuming that the blonde was alone in the house? He burned to pick up the extension he could see just inside a large reception room, but did not dare. The click of the receiver being lifted would be a dead giveaway and the police could be summoned by one or both parties on the line before he could get up the stairs and silence the blonde.

Hunger drove him onwards. To the back of the house where, with luck and if this house conformed to the usual floor plans of such houses, he would find the kitchen. He had eaten nothing for hours except the block of stale chocolate he had buried with the parcel. Probably it had been as well that his sense of taste had been dulled by excitement and fatigue. But now he was ravenously hungry.

The door at the end of the hallway was right. He stepped into a kitchen which reflected light from every gleaming white surface. Enough to strike a man snow-blind – just what you'd expect in a house like this.

Blinking, he looked around. It took him only a second to locate the refrigerator – a large white oblong in a corner emitting a low rumble, like the purr of a contented cat. He crossed the room swiftly and yanked open the door, forgetting the need for silence in his more urgent need for sustenance.

It wasn't as full as he'd hoped it would be. Probably the house was only occupied week-ends. There was a partially-consumed chicken, glazed with the peculiar colour that betrayed that it had been purchased ready-cooked; two and a half pints of milk; a polythene bowl half full of limp delicatessen salad; three eggs on a dish, presumably hard-boiled, since six other eggs were dispersed along the neat little mouldings built into the door of the fridge; a wedge of cheese; butter; and that was it.

It was enough. With what was evidently an emergency departure imminent, it was unlikely that anyone was going to take an inventory of the contents of the fridge. Nevertheless, rudimentary caution was called for. He took one of the eggs from the plate and tapped it lightly on the metal shelf and brushed away part of the shell. As he had thought, it was hard-boiled. He took a second egg, replacing them with two raw eggs from the door – a cursory glance was all that the fridge was likely to get, if that, before the helicopter arrived. He tore off a leg of chicken and carefully tilted the chicken over on to its opposite side so that the loss would not be immediately apparent. He broke off a chunk of cheese, turned the dish around and moved it towards the back of the fridge.

There was a sharp hiss behind him and he whirled about, aiming his gun at the source. But it was only the kettle beginning to boil.

He hovered between a laugh and a curse, but uttered neither. He crossed to the stove and turned the gas as low as it could be set without actually going out. For a moment, he looked longingly at the waiting cups on the table, but that would take time and was dangerous. He could not afford time when the telephone conversation upstairs might finish at any moment and leave the blonde free to start roaming through the house again. It was she who had left the kettle on – she would head directly for the kitchen.

Reluctantly he returned to the fridge and took a bottle of the chilled milk. Cold, but nourishing – and

portable – that was the main essential right now. The
bottle might or might not be missed. That would have
to be risked.

He closed the fridge door and looked around. Bread
would be nice, but was an unnecessary luxury. No
breadbox was in sight and he could not spare the time
to go rootling through cupboards in the hope of finding
some. Besides, from the brief glimpse he had had of the
occupants of this house, they might be on the kind of
diet that dispensed with bread altogether.

There was movement upstairs. His preternaturally
alert ears caught the sound of footsteps moving across a
carpeted room. The telephone conversation must be at
an end, and it was time for him to get out of sight – for
the moment.

He moved towards the door he had marked as an
exit route. From all his experience, it would lead to a
cellar. He could sit on the stairs, eat his picnic lunch,
and wait for the arrival of the helicopter before making
his next move. Resisting temptation all the while.

For, in this sort of house, it was bound to be a wine
cellar.

CHAPTER XI

Genevieve shut the door, almost on his heels. She
wasn't going to stand there and watch him go. Those
days were over. There had been too many of them. Too
many departure lounges, too many railway stations,
even, in the earlier days, too many hours spent at
dockside watching a ship glide down the St Lawrence

Seaway until, finally, the river carried it out of sight. Too many goodbyes.

Until, finally, she had realized that she was more familiar with Paul's back view moving away from her than with his face coming towards her. Gradually, his visits had become briefer, his absences more prolonged.

Her grandmother had been dead by then. That had been her main regret. Gran Marie would have understood. In fact, Gran Marie had warned her of it back in the days when she had first begun going out with Paul. Even at the expense of hearing her say, '*I told you so*', she had still wished that Gran Marie could have been there. No one else could have understood so well.

'*He is English?*' Gran Marie had shaken her head forebodingly at the news. '*It will come to no good, then. You must forget him. Look for a man among your own people. To an Englishman, you will never be anything more than a winter wife.*'

Because she had listened to the stories of Gran Marie's girlhood all her life, Genevieve had discounted Gran Marie's prejudices and made allowances for them. Perhaps she should have listened. History had a habit of repeating itself.

Just before the First World War, Gran Marie – barely into her teens – had slipped across the US-Canadian border with a friend, both determined to make their fortunes down in a richer land where the streets were well known to be paved with gold.

But the facts had proved disillusioning and Gran Marie and her friend had been glad to find refuge as lower-echelon servants in the home of a wealthy Anglo-American textile merchant who owned factories in the mill towns of Lawrence and Lowell, in Massachusetts, and made frequent trips across the Atlantic – without his wife and family – to the rival mill towns in Lancashire.

They were business trips, he claimed, to see what the competition was doing, and to try to steal the best men. In fact, to hire many men cheaply for the American mills when the English mills were passing through a time of depression.

Unpacking after one of those trips had been a chore best not spoken of – especially to the ladies of the household. Shirts tainted with strange scents and tinted face powders. Lace-edged handkerchiefs tucked into suit pockets and forgotten. Stubs of theatre tickets – for two.

'*Like master, like men,*' Gran Marie had said darkly.

For the millhands, also, had sought their home comforts in a country so far from their real homes. Especially the ones who had made a regular practice of sailing between the Massachusetts and the Lancashire mill towns, moving from one country to the other as the work slacked off in one and picked up in the other.

'*A winter wife and a summer wife – with families to match.*' Neither suspecting the existence of the other or, at least, not questioning. Legitimacy was only important when there was a question of inheritance. Millhands would have nothing to leave. Itinerant workers, crossing an ocean as casually as farm labourers crossed state lines in search of work, they supported their families as best they could – when they were there; and, when they weren't there, the wives went out to work, either in the mills, or as servants in the big houses.

No, better not to question. But there had been

rumours, girls in tears, men who disappeared at the
end of one season and did not return again. Women
who had never been sure whether they were wives or
widows – or had never been wives at all. Yet other
girls 'walked out' with visiting millhands, certain that
such a betrayal could never happen to them, positive
that *their* man was free and unencumbered and would
remain with them – or come back to them.

But not Gran Marie. She had watched it happen to
too many other girls and her French-Canadian distrust
of the English had been reinforced by their experiences.
Let the little mill girls laugh at her foreign ways and
call her 'Canuck', she worked hard, saved her money,
accumulated a respectable *dot*, and married her
Etienne, a lumberjack.

When Etienne had had an accident breaking up a
log jam in the river soon after their marriage, the *dot*
and the insurance money had combined to buy a small
lumber yard and carpentry shop in the Old Town of
Quebec. The business had grown and flourished,
providing the means of raising and educating a family
and placing Gran Marie and Etienne firmly among the
petit bourgeoisie of the province. From which eminence,
Gran Marie had always looked askance on the English
and their ways, and never ceased to warn her children
and grandchildren of the dangers of having anything
to do with perfidious Englishmen.

Genevieve had been the only one who had not
heeded the warning. And now she was about to pay the
price for that. '*Inevitable price*,' Gran Marie would
have said with that familiar shake of her head.

There was the ghost of a whimper from above.
Genevieve turned and rushed upstairs, but Sandy was

still sleeping lightly although shadows crossing her face and the faint whimper suggested that the pain was increasing again.

Let her sleep as long as she could. Time enough to try to dress her when the pain forced her awake. Every moment she could remain unaware of it was a moment nearer the time when the helicopter would arrive to lift her to London and proper medical help.

As silently as possible, Genevieve began pulling out the warmest clothing she could find in readiness for Sandy's awakening. A blanket, too, would be a good idea. And she must set the kettle to boil again so that the hot-water bottle could be refilled at the last possible moment in order to retain its comforting heat throughout the journey.

'*Mum-mee* . . .' Sandy whimpered, not quite conscious, not quite asleep.

'Shh-shh . . .' Genevieve rushed to her side and stroked her forehead. 'Go back to sleep. It's all right. Don't wake up. Shh-shh . . . I'll sing you a lullaby. Remember how you loved this when you were just a little girl?'

'*Frère Jacques, Frère Jacques,*
'*Dormez-vous, dormez-vous . . .*'

Surely, the helicopter must arrive soon.

CHAPTER XII

Lillian pushed open the kitchen door and halted abruptly, discovering in herself a strange reluctance to proceed any further. The kitchen was as brightly lit as she had left it, but there seemed a chill air about it. Perhaps the fog was beginning to creep in from outside, or perhaps it was that, in the absence of Paul, the whole house had seemed to become colder, less comfortable. It was as though the house were drawing in on itself, shutting her out, recognizing her as an intruder.

Yes, it was definitely Genevieve's house – and Genevieve must have it. She and Paul would start over again in a new house, one of their own, preferably in another county.

The reaffirmation of her earlier decision steadied her. She moved forward, trying to pull her thoughts away from the dangerous territory and centre them on the current problem and the task in hand. Which was to make coffee and fill the Thermos flask for the journey ahead, and also to make sandwiches. There would be no restaurants open in the City until long after they had arrived and it was unthinkable that Paul should have to face the Extraordinary General Meeting without having had something to eat.

Lillian crossed the kitchen, frowning faintly, but unable to put forth a solid reason for her increasing uneasiness. Perhaps she was receiving some sort of extra-sensory emanations from Paul. He might have found little Alexandra worse than he had feared when he reached Dower House Cottage. But, in that case, wouldn't he have telephoned her?

Or was it possible that she could feel any concern for the child on her own account? Before long, Alexandra would be her step-daughter, a ready-made member of what ought to be a new family unit, someone to be absorbed for holiday visits, a strange new relationship to try to make viable. Could she succeed, or would the child always secretly hate her?

It was a question she had hitherto avoided contemplating. But it was coming closer with every passing day. She was unaccustomed to children. If she had ever thought about them at all, she had automatically assumed that she would become accustomed by the natural process of having one of her own, living with it from the beginning, watching it grow, shaping and moulding a young life as it developed. It had never occurred to her she would one day have to take on a semi-grown daughter she had never seen before.

And yet, Sandy was a sweet child. Perhaps, under other circumstances, they would have liked each other more. Circumstances in which she did not appear as the villainess, the woman who had taken Daddy away from Mummy. Children saw things in black and white, unable to deal with the complexities of shades of grey. They could not understand the emotional turmoil of three basically decent adults who had been caught in an age-old trap which was, essentially, no one's fault.

But what if something should happen to Sandy? What if the helicopter didn't arrive in time? If the appendix ruptured out here in the wilds beyond medical help? What, then, would happen to their relationship, with Paul haunted by guilt for the rest of his life? And what would she herself feel, knowing that the child would never have been in this country were it not that the adults were trying to work out the property settlements necessary to the divorce proceedings?

But she was letting her imagination slip out of control. Lillian swept the shadows firmly from her mind, looking around the kitchen, as though for another light to snap to illumine the dark crevices of her consciousness and dispel the fears. Harlow, while not likeable, was thoroughly dependable, so the helicopter was safely on the way, Sandy would soon be comfortable in a hospital bed, and the Extraordinary General Meeting would get under way with Paul firmly in control and remaining so.

There was nothing to worry about and no sense in borrowing trouble. Concentrate on the present, and take that present one step at a time.

First, the coffee. She crossed to the cupboard for the jar of instant coffee – there wouldn't be time to bother with the percolator. Instant would be good enough. It wasn't required for gourmet purposes, just for caffeine and warmth.

Swiftly she spooned coffee powder into the Thermos flask, turned to take the kettle off the hob, then hesitated uneasily. Surely, she had left the gas higher than *that*? She lifted the kettle and stared down at the pale yellow tongues barely flickering from the jets around the ring. Perhaps the gas pressure had been reduced?

No. She touched the control knob and the flames immediately hissed higher. The pressure was normal. Strange. Perhaps she had been mistaken. No. She distinctly recalled that she had left the gas turned moderately high when she went upstairs, knowing that that would encourage her to keep her call to Harlow brief. It was possible, of course, that the control knob was faulty and the gas had gradually slipped down from whatever height it had been turned to.

With a mental shrug, Lillian turned the gas off completely and left the kettle there to come off the boil before she poured the water into the Thermos. The gas cooker, like everything else in the house, would soon be Genevieve's. There was no point in worrying about any inadequacies it might be developing. They would be Genevieve's problem soon.

Dismissing the thought, she opened the fridge and brought out the chicken and the bowl of hard-boiled eggs, then took the loaf of bread from the breadbox and began slicing it. There was only enough for a few sandwiches – they had been going into town for fresh supplies in the morning – but she wasn't hungry and doubted that Paul was. However, he must have something to eat before the meeting and it would make a breakfast of sorts. In any case, it gave her something to do while she waited for Paul to come back.

She buttered the few slices of bread and turned to the chicken. It slid towards her on the plate, seeming curiously light. As she turned it to carve, the far side was exposed – what was left of it. The drumstick was missing and the flesh higher up was rough and shredded as though a large chunk had been ripped away. Yet that side of the chicken had been untouched when she put it into the fridge earlier tonight – last night.

Paul? Paul, succumbing to the urge towards compulsive eating that sometimes characterized periods of stress in people? Paul, slipping downstairs for a mid-

night snack without her knowledge? Without mention-
ing it to her? Or without her having noticed?

Not that there was any reason why he should have
mentioned it – he was perfectly entitled to help himself
to anything he wanted from the fridge. Yet they had
both had a very good supper and she was certain that
he could not really have been hungry. It seemed most
unlike him, but it was, she supposed, possible.

The alternative was mice. With a faint smile, she
reached out and took up one of the hard-boiled eggs,
tapping it absently on the table to crack the shell.
Nothing happened and she tapped harder.

The shell abruptly disintegrated, plunging her hand
downwards into a glutinous mass. She stopped smiling
and stared down incredulously at the mess on the table
top. It was impossible. She had hard-boiled those eggs
herself and placed them in that bowl. What was going
on here?

Could Paul be playing some sort of practical joke?
That, too, was unlike him. Of course, he might have
started it before those telephone calls. But the atmosphere had not been so light-hearted even then. Not
with the discussions with Genevieve hanging over
them.

Furthermore, Paul was not the joking type. He had
a sense of humour, of course, but it was expressed in
words. Words which, she realized, were becoming
increasingly wry and sardonic as time went on.
Especially in this last year.

Considering it, she went to the sink, ran cold water
over her hands and took a paper towel to clean up the
egg. Working automatically, she let her mind worry
this new insight. Perhaps because it was easier to

encompass at this moment than the minor mysteries in the kitchen which was not really hers.

Surely, when she had first gone to work for Paul, he had been a more open, higher-spirited man. Was the growing change in him due solely to the increasing responsibilities that went with his international commitments, or was it in part due to the strains in his private life? But she had been instrumental in easing many of those strains.

It had been Genevieve, with her refusal to leave Canada and settle in England, who had been responsible for much of the strain. Genevieve, keeping Sandy with her, using Sandy's schooling as the excuse for not being with Paul. A house divided —

The house — *this* house. Lillian lifted her head, straining her ears to listen, as though the house could tell her something if only she could interpret the creaks and groans of its shifting wood correctly.

Her mind, released from its preoccupation with Paul, darted back to worry at the strangenesses she had discovered. Genevieve? Genevieve still possessed keys to this house. Had she come over, entered under cover of the darkness and the fog, and — ?

And played silly practical jokes? Leaving her child alone in Dower House Cottage? Her sick child? Even if she had not known Sandy was ailing, it was impossible.

There must be an explanation — and Paul would be able to give it to her when he returned.

If he returned.

That was another thought she did not want to face.

If he did not return soon, it would mean that Sandy was worse, far worse, than they had feared. It would mean that he did not want to leave Genevieve alone with her. It would mean . . . perhaps . . . that the helicopter might come too late . . .

No! She would not think of things like that! She hurled the carving knife down on the table. It fell with a clatter – and there was an answering echo just beyond the cellar door.

She turned towards the sound, abruptly tense and suspicious. Her nerves were on edge, she assured herself as she moved towards the cellar door. Then she hesitated and stretched out her hand, taking up the carving knife again. Some remnant of normalcy deep within her consciousness began to laugh at her – but not with enough conviction to make her lay down the knife again.

It might not be enough protection. It might be no protection at all. She knew the argument and theories: any weapon could be wrenched away from you and used against you. Therefore, it was better to have no weapon at all. Theoretically.

Just let the theorists stand alone in a hostile house with strange noises beaming at them from every direction! If *she* went down, she was going down fighting. Stealthily, she advanced upon the cellar door. Was that door just slightly ajar?

She hesitated, gripping the carving knife more tightly. Neither she nor Paul had been anywhere near the cellar since they had arrived. Surely the door should still be securely latched?

Or had it been latched to begin with? She could not say. She had paid no attention to trifles like that. There had been too many other problems to consider – there still were.

Was her imagination building mountains out of molehills in a matey attempt to keep her from worrying too much over the very real problems life contained right now? Had she *really* heard any sound at all behind that door?

As she wavered, there was suddenly a sharp and clear-cut sound about which there could be no doubt. The front-door latch.

'Paul!' She whirled about and dashed into the front hall then halted.

A stranger faced her. Careworn, his shoulders drooping, he looked years older than he had when he left the house such a short time ago. He raised his head and, seeing her, forced a smile.

'Paul!' She rushed forward into his arms.

CHAPTER XIII

Dower House seemed strange and unfamiliar to Paul Jarvis as he closed the door behind him. Not that Dower House Cottage had seemed any more of a home or refuge. He felt immeasurably older and yet his mind seemed to have reverted to earlier days and it seemed to him that somewhere there must be a doorway through which he could walk – if only he could find it – to emerge into the crisp clear Canadian air of yesterday. Yesterday, when life had been so much less complicated, when his ambitions were still dreams and the fulfilment of them foreshadowed none of the problems which had actually ensued.

What was he doing here ricocheting between two

women, each of whom he loved and was bound to in a different way? What had happened to the young Paul? Who was the desperate-eyed woman he had just left behind him in Dower House Cottage? Who was this wild-eyed woman in front of him brandishing a kinfe? *Brandishing a knife?*

'Lillian!' He caught her as she hurtled into his arms and gently detached the carving knife from her hand. 'Lillian – what's the matter?'

'Nothing.' She clung to him, half-laughing. 'It's all right – now that you're here.' She pushed herself away from him and looked up into his face, seeming to realize that just a little more explanation was required.

'I was just . . . all alone here . . . I was cutting sandwiches and . . .'

'Good idea,' he said approvingly, although he had no interest in food and felt that he might never have any such interest again. It would keep her occupied.

'Yes, but – ' She frowned. 'Paul, it's rather strange. Did you, by any chance – ?'

'Did you put all the relevant papers in my briefcase?' He didn't mean to cut her off so abruptly, but time was short. They could explore the 'by any chances' at some future time.

'Of course.' She snapped back into being the superefficient Miss Duxworthy again.

'You've been in touch with Harlow?'

'Everything is under control at that end. The helicopter ought to be here – ' she glanced at her watch – 'any minute now.'

'Good,' he said automatically, only a portion of his attention on what she was saying. The rest remained centred on that small still form whimpering in pain back at Dower House Cottage. Yet another part of his mind was still teasing at the memories of long ago, wondering what had gone wrong.

Was that the way it was with Genevieve? Had she had these feelings all along?

With an effort, he pulled his mind away. There was no profit in second-guessing when it was too late to do anything about it. Furthermore, it was dangerous to the future to be distracted by the past right now. He needed all his attention concentrated on the Extraordinary General Meeting ahead. It would take all his concentration and force of will to get through that and come out on the winning side. He knew the guns that were being massed against him; once he had won, he would see that they were spiked permanently. They knew that, too, and that was why it was going to be a fight to the finish. It had been on the cards for some time, but he had not really expected it to happen for perhaps another five years. It had come at the worst possible time.

But he mustn't start thinking about that again. All the necessary machinery had been set in motion. Everything possible was being done for Sandy. As soon as the helicopter arrived, that part of the problem would be over. The hospital had been alerted, the helicopter would light down in Coram's Fields and transfer Sandy to a waiting ambulance and the operation – if one were necessary – would be over in no time. Probably long before his own Boardroom battle was over.

'Is Sandy . . . ? How is she?' Lillian asked hesitantly, as though sensing the distance that had come between them.

'She's holding on. She'll be all right.' He smiled at

Lillian with reassuring warmth, unwilling to let her realize that she had become, however momentarily, a stranger to him. 'She comes of good, tough stock.'

'Yes.' Lillian's expression was half-smile, half-wince, and he cursed himself. All roads led back to Genevieve. Yet Sandy was *his* daughter, too. Was it always to be like this between them?

'Would you like a cup of coffee?' Lillian made a frantic effort to retrieve the situation. 'The kettle's boiling.'

'Fine,' he said, too heartily. There was nothing he really wanted – except to be on his way, but Lillian had nothing else to offer at the moment.

Lillian smiled, turning towards the kitchen. He set the knife down on the hall table and started towards the stairs. She looked back over her shoulder and halted abruptly.

'Where are you going?' There was a trace of something he had never heard before in her voice. Could it have been panic?

'I just want to check a couple of things,' he said reassuringly. 'You make the coffee. I'll be down in a minute.'

'I'll come with you,' she said quickly. She moved to follow him, hesitated at the hall table and stretched out her hand for the knife.

'You won't need *that*,' he said. Instantly, he realized that he might have sounded too welcoming. He tried to undo it with an abstracted frown.

'You'd better stay down here,' he said, 'and finish up in the kitchen.' It was the wrong thing to say, her face told him that. But there was no right comment in this situation. He needed a few moments to himself desperately. Just a spell of solitude – however brief – before the world closed in on him again.

It was increasingly being borne in upon his consciousness that he was committed to an indefinite stretch of time in the company of the two women in his life. How long would the flight take – an hour, two hours? During that time, however subtly, their psyches would batter at his own. They would be vying for his attention, trying to assert their claims, to score each other off, to prove something – God knew what – to themselves and to each other. Perhaps to him, too.

All he needed. He mounted the stairs swiftly, not looking back, hoping she would take the hint. He *had* to have some time to himself. Perhaps she recognized that fact; there were no following footsteps on the stairs. After all, Lillian had been a secretary first – and a good one – her sensitivity to his moods had been one of the major factors in the development of their relationship.

'I'll be right down,' he said.

'I'll have the coffee ready.'

At the top, he risked a backward glance. Lillian was still lingering at the foot of the stairs – and she was still clutching the carving knife.

CHAPTER XIV

Close. That had been very close.

He relaxed his grip on the gun, but did not replace it in his belt. There were two of them in the house now, the danger was doubled. What were they saying to each other out there in the hallway?

He risked edging the door wider open, but the faint sound of conversation was no clearer. Wider still, and he applied his eye to the crack cautiously. No one in sight. The food on the kitchen table was clearly visible and his stomach gave a faint rumble.

He leaped back and closed the door again, leaving just the hairline opening. Things had been going so well for him that he must not risk premature discovery. He was warm: there had been a pullover smelling of woodsmoke hanging on the back of the cellar door, and he had donned it. By the time some handyman or gardener discovered the loss, he would be safely away. And, although he still felt vaguely hungry, he had had food. He had eaten the chicken leg and dropped the bone over the stairs into the cellar. Now he took an egg from his pocket, crushed the shell one-handed and slipped it off, tossing the shell after the chicken bone. The egg would have tasted better with a bit of salt and pepper, but it would be foolhardy to try to take anything from the kitchen table and risk exposing his presence at this moment. Surprise was the biggest element on his side right now.

But why had the woman suddenly started prowling around the kitchen carrying that knife? Had something made her suspicious?

The chicken, of course. She had noticed the missing piece. You wouldn't expect people in a place like this to keep track of food like that. But of course that was how they got places like this. Probably counted every mouthful the servants ate and had done so for generations back. It was bred into them. Especially the women. Cheese-paring bitches!

It was a pity she hadn't thrown open the cellar door and discovered him. He could have taken that knife away from her and really taught her how to use it.

His fingers clenched involuntarily and the remaining bit of hard-boiled egg spun out of them and fell away into the darkness. Mustn't get excited. Mustn't think about things like that. Need a clear head.

He took a deep breath and closed his eyes, forcing the images to fade away before it got to be the way the prison trick-cyclist had explained to him: old thoughts triggering off the old behavioural patterns.

He grinned wryly. *Behavioural patterns* – a nice new classy name for an old-fashioned act like killing.

But this was a time to concentrate on the present. The next few hours were the ones to see him through to freedom and a new life in another part of the world. Let the old behavioural patterns wait until then.

Meanwhile, the house had gone silent. No more murmur of voices from the front hall. Why had they stopped talking? Could they have left the house to await the helicopter outside? Or might they both have gone to the other house? Why was it so silent?

This time he squinted through the keyhole, which was aligned with the kitchen table. The sight of the waiting food reassured him. The woman, at least, would not have gone off and left food uncovered on the table. She had been in the process of packing some sort of picnic lunch – little realizing who she was actually packing it for.

She must come back, sooner or later, to finish the job. When she did, he would be waiting.

CHAPTER XV

Paul Jarvis shut the bedroom door firmly behind him –
just in case Lillian might be tempted to follow him
upstairs. He hoped that it would be sufficiently dis-
couraging. If not, then he might have to tell her bluntly
that he wanted to be alone for a few minutes.

Yet he knew he couldn't do that to her. She had been
showing signs of increasing insecurity recently. Since
Genevieve had arrived in this country, in fact. It seemed
to make no difference that the reason for Genevieve's
presence was to thrash out the property settlement.
Intellectually, Lillian realized that; emotionally, she
still reacted as though Genevieve were some sort of
threat to her.

Or was it Sandy who was the root cause of the
trouble? In that case, what could be done? It would be
easy enough to arrange life in the future so that Lillian
need never meet Genevieve again, but he was not going
to cut his only child out of his life. He would see as
much of her as Genevieve allowed, although he fore-
saw Genevieve trying to fight some of his plans for
Sandy. In time, he hoped that Sandy would come to
spend summer holidays in England with them,
perhaps even choose to go to an English university,
Oxford or Cambridge, in preference to McGill or
Toronto or any of the American ones open to her. That
would mean that Sandy could come 'home' for week-
ends, as well as holidays, and truly become part of their
lives.

That was what he had been hoping would happen. But how could it if Lillian felt genuine animosity towards the child? He tried to tell himself that he was imagining things. He could not see Lillian in the classic 'wicked stepmother' situation. Yet neither had he ever envisaged that he and Genevieve would come to the parting of the ways as they had. Was part of his problem that he saw people as he wished they were, not as they actually were?

Certainly, he had been over-optimistic about the Board of Directors, not foreseeing that they would make their takeover attempt so soon. That, too, was part of his problem – and the part he should be thinking about right now. Let the rest of it await him in that amorphous future looming indistinctly ahead. Time enough to sort it out when it actually caught up with him.

He opened his briefcase and checked the contents. Everything was there and in order. He should not have doubted Lillian. He didn't doubt her – and yet, he just wanted to make sure. Was he losing his ability to delegate?

Or was his own basic insecurity beginning to show through? If so, it was one hell of a time for that to happen, with the Extraordinary General Meeting due to convene in just a few hours.

Paul snapped the briefcase shut in a decisive gesture and looked around the room. It showed little sign of having been occupied. Lillian's overnight case was packed and waiting by the door. She insisted on packing it and bringing it each time, although he had repeatedly suggested that she leave a personal wardrobe down here, as he did, so that it would not be necessary.

Insecurity again? Or was it indicative of some deeper unrest? Lillian had already made a tentative suggestion that they allow Genevieve to keep this property and find another house for themselves. Could it be that she did not like the house? Because it was too big? Or because it had been another woman's first? But so had he. Perhaps it was better not to follow that thought too far.

He set his briefcase down beside the overnight case and considered. Ought he to take an extra blanket for Sandy? Or would Genevieve think of that and consider it a slight if he did so? Would she be upset? Hurt?

Indecision gripped him again.

He could not go on like this! Angry with himself, he crossed to the window and looked out. The fog had blotted out earth and sky alike. The lights of Dower House Cottage were no longer visible, the cottage itself entirely obliterated. He stared in the direction he knew it to be, feeling disorientated by the sudden absence of familiar landmarks. It was the sort of night on which one could believe in omens; a superstitious dread rose in him even as his conscious mind mocked the thought.

Yet it was not so far out: the fog was not the omen, the fog was the threat.

Could the helicopter land and take off safely through that solid cotton-wool menace? If not, what chance was there for Sandy?

He moved forward and opened the window, leaning out into the thick of the mist. Still the sky was not to be seen. Only the heavy wet fog roiling above him as it roiled below. He might be alone in the void, poised between heaven and hell, in some nightmare from which there was no awakening.

With a shudder, he pulled himself back into the brightness of the room and retreated from the window. He shuddered again and pulled a spare blanket from the chest at the foot of the bed. An extra blanket would not come amiss on a night like this. He draped it over his arm and hesitated.

He should go back and close the window, but something within him shrank from doing so, as though the wisps of fog already drifting into the room were tentacles which would wrap around him and drag him out into the murk.

He gave himself a mental shake. It was not like him to deal in fantasies. Facts and balance sheets were his normal range. It had been years since he had let his imagination roam far from them. He must not let his attention keep wandering tonight – this morning. There was too much at stake.

He opened the door and snapped off the light, anxious now to go back downstairs. Solitude had abruptly lost its attraction for him.

CHAPTER XVI

Loitering with intent, Lillian thought, watching Paul's retreating back. She longed to call after him, to ask how long he'd be, or to tell him to hurry, but she forced herself to keep silent. The uncompromising set of his shoulders warned her that he was likely to have little patience with feminine foibles at the moment. It was not the time to make herself look silly in his eyes.

She turned towards the kitchen and hesitated. She *felt* silly, but she did not want to go back into that kitchen alone.

At least, she should have asked Paul about the chicken. But how could she? He had looked suddenly like a stranger when he came through the door. He had *been* a stranger.

He had stood there looking at her as though she were an unsatisfactory job applicant. One who was so definitely unsuitable for the position that he would subsequently dictate a stiff letter of complaint to the agency, pointing out that they were wasting his valuable time by sending along such substandard material.

She could not have raised such an intimate question at such a moment. It had taken all her courage to enquire about Sandy. Even then, he had changed the subject in a way that relegated her back into the persona of Miss Duxworthy, Executive Secretary.

What had happened to Lillian? Last night had suddenly seemed very far away.

Why was life so complex? Why couldn't she have fallen in love with one of the nice, uncomplicated, *dull* young men she had met along the way?

Why was she standing here asking herself stupid questions instead of going back into the kitchen?

Sheer funk was not a satisfactory answer. It was certainly one Paul would never accept from one of his staff. Far less from his intended wife. She was not even willing to accept it from herself.

Determinedly she straightened her shoulders and turned. Without giving the dark corners of her consciousness any time to raise further protests, she marched down the hallway and into the kitchen.

She still did not like it here. She still had the scream-ing atavistic impulse to turn and run. Screaming.

And what would Paul say to that?

She flinched from the mental picture of him charging down the stairs, rushing to her aid, and finding . . . nothing.

She took a deep unsteady breath and held it while her eyes searched the empty kitchen . . . finding nothing.

She moved slowly into the centre of the room, still clutching the carving knife defensively. Nothing hindered her progress; nothing threatened her. The room was silent and neutral. She had been imagining things.

Imagination. Nerves. Intuition? Paul had little patience with any of those things.

Ordinarily she hadn't herself.

Nor did a City office offer much scope for them. In times of crisis, the sharp ring of a telephone or the sud-den chatter of the Telex were of more immediate and sinister portent than things that went bump in the night. She wished that she were back there now.

She soon would be.

The thought comforted her. As did the knowledge of Paul's presence upstairs.

Moving cautiously, she returned to her self-ap-pointed task and finished the sandwiches, replacing the thoroughly depleted chicken carcass in the fridge. Tomorrow she would ring the woman in the village to come and clean the house and tidy everything away before she and Paul paid another visit.

Perhaps – the thought cheered her – Genevieve

would elect to remain in London for a while. If Sandy *were* in need of an appendicectomy, that would require several days' stay in hospital and Genevieve would want to be near her. Perhaps they could sort out the settlement in London rather than come down here again.

Also, Paul might be needed in London for longer than he anticipated. If the Boardroom rebellion had got this far, there could be more to unpick than he envisaged. Certainly there would be fences to mend.

She still had not turned her back on the cellar door. It was not a conscious decision – to admit that would be to admit how certain she was that something was wrong. And if she were that certain, then she had no excuse for not telling Paul – even though he might deride her.

The alternative, of course, was to open the cellar door and see for herself that there was nothing there. Or that there was.

Did she really want to know?

They would be out of here soon. Safely back in London. Leave the house to itself and its own secrets. Let Genevieve discover them at some point in the future. They were nothing to do with her. Nor with Paul.

Everything was ready now. The lunch packed and in the small basket ready to be carried to the helicopter. The two cups and saucers stood on the table, waiting for Paul to come downstairs. What was taking him so long?

She had time to investigate. Plenty of time, and Paul within calling distance. Hesitantly she edged a little closer to the cellar door. If she were to be a dramatic fool and throw it open suddenly, better to do it now without any witness if nothing were there to be discovered –

There was a sudden thunderous clatter directly overhead. For a moment, she thought Paul must have dropped something upstairs, then she realized that it must be the helicopter.

Another, lighter clatter sounded from the front hall as Paul's footsteps hurried down the stairs. Everything else forgotten, she went to meet him.

'Take these.' He thrust the briefcase and her own overnight case at her. He carried a folded blanket over his arm. 'I'll meet you at the helicopter.' He opened the front door.

'You're not coming with me?' She had known that he must go back to Genevieve, yet she felt a sudden chill.

'Sorry, we haven't time for two trips. And I'll have to carry Sandy. Genevieve can't manage on her own.'

And I can. With an effort, she kept the comment unspoken. It might sound too much like nagging. And it wasn't fair. Of course Genevieve needed help with a sick child. Paul was right to go.

'I'll explain our change of plan to the pilot,' Lillian offered in apology. 'He'll have to plot a new course to land Sandy first.'

'Good girl.' Paul gave her a brief, unseeing smile and strode away without a backward glance.

She watched him go, swallowed up in the soft white maw of the devouring fog in just a few steps.

Lillian sighed faintly and turned back into the waiting house.

CHAPTER XVII

Even waiting, hoping, listening for the first far-off sound to herald the approaching helicopter, Genevieve had mistaken it at first for the erratic clamour of her own heart.

Sandy was worse, she knew it. Semi-conscious, but beyond complaining, Sandy lay listless, only her eyes moving to follow her mother's progress around the room as Genevieve packed the few items that would be needed for a hospital stay.

Fearing to rouse her into full consciousness by too much noise or activity, Genevieve moved slowly and casually, concentrating on packing the barest minimum. Anything else necessary could be purchased in London.

When the abrupt explosion of sound erupted overhead, Sandy whimpered, tossing her head from side to side.

'It's all right, *chérie.*' Genevieve rushed to her. 'That's help arriving. We'll be in London soon . . . Here, let me put your shoes and stockings on.'

Sandy resisted feebly, kicking out against the restriction of superfluous clothing. 'No!'

'*Chérie, chérie,*' Genevieve soothed. 'Just slide your toes in . . . that's right. You cannot go up to London in bare feet like a little peasant girl in your great-grandmother's time . . .'

'Don't want to go to London.' Sandy was more awake now. 'Don't want to move.' Her agitation was increasing. 'It hurts to move. Want to stay here.'

'You cannot, *chérie*.' Half-sobbing herself, Genevieve struggled to slide a stocking over a wriggling foot. 'You *must* go to London. The doctors there will make you well again. They will stop the hurt.'

'Don't . . . don't . . .'

'Shh, shh, *chérie*. It won't take long. We'll be there before you know it. And we're going in a helicopter! What do you think of that? You've never ridden in one of those before, have you?'

Interest flared for an instant in the lacklustre eyes, then Sandy pulled away and doubled up as another spasm of pain convulsed her. 'No,' she moaned. 'Go away.'

Thankfully Genevieve heard the slam of the front door. Paul was back.

'Up here,' she called.

'Daddy?' Again, Sandy roused to a flicker of healthy animation. Her head turned eagerly towards the door.

'Here he is, *chérie*.' She had never been so glad to see Paul before. Well, not for a long, long time.

'Here we are, sweetheart.' Paul strode over to the bed, taking in the situation at a glance.

'Don't bother about those.' He pushed Genevieve's hand away with the stockings. 'We can put them on later. Right now, let's get going.'

'Daddy,' Sandy protested feebly. 'Don't want to go . . .'

'Of course you want to go, sweetheart.' Deftly he wrapped the blanket around her and swung her up into his arms.

'No-o-o . . .' Still shaking her head, Sandy twined her arms around his neck and clung to him.

'You'll feel better when we're in the lovely helicopter,' Genevieve promised recklessly. She turned out the bedroom light and followed them downstairs, snapping off the lights along the way, and out of the door.

'That's right,' Paul promised, with more certainty. 'As soon as we get into the air, all our troubles will be over.'

CHAPTER XVIII

He had opened the cellar door again, just enough to follow the progress of the couple in the front hall. Their words were unclear, but there had been a finality in the man's voice and then the slam of the front door.

After that, the woman came back slowly into the kitchen. Alone.

The rhythmic clatter of the helicopter's rotors throbbed like a purposeful heartbeat outside. It had obviously set down quite near the house. Would the pilot report at the door?

He kept his eye to the slightly wider crack looking into the kitchen, emboldened now that the man had left the house.

The woman worked swiftly, not glancing in his direction. Her earlier suspicion seemed allayed; or perhaps she too was emboldened. The thought of imminent departure had obviously put all minor considerations out of her mind. She had even begun humming softly. So much the better, it would help him to keep track of her when she moved out of sight.

He waited until she had gathered everything together and snapped off the light before emerging from the cellar entrance and following her silently. She paused in the front hallway to collect a couple of cases. He waited patiently while she worked out the best way of balancing all that she had to carry. It had been unlikely in any event that she would put up much of a struggle. Laden as she now was, it would be impossible for her. Added to which, of course, he had the element of surprise in his favour.

She went down the hallway ahead of him, snapping off the lights in the rooms along the way, as she had turned them on in that earlier progress he had also watched. She moved quickly, happily, anxious to be out of this house and away to some more pleasant destination. Silently he padded after her.

She snapped off the last lights, the hall light itself and, after a momentary pause, the light outside over the front door.

'Right.' He moved forward to face her as she turned back to shut the front door, letting her see the gun. 'Just keep quiet and keep moving.'

CHAPTER XIX

Carson gave himself a breather after setting down the helicopter and sliding open the door in readiness for passengers to board. Incredible to look around what he had been told was a tennis court and remember that, just a few hundred feet above, there was a clear moon-lit sky. Pea-soup fog was truly well named.

It was not a phenomenon he had encountered often. When the weather was as bad as this, you just didn't take off. Rule books and instructors were adamant on that. *'I didn't raise my boy to be a soldier'* . . . and the Army didn't train their helicopter pilots to take unnecessary risks. More because several hundred thousand pounds' worth of machinery could be at risk than because they were concerned about their boy's neck. The boy had to worry about his own neck.

At the moment that was just what Carson was doing.

Getting down here had been bad enough. And now he had to wrestle this hulk back to London with a human cargo aboard. VIPs and, with his kind of luck, they'd both be back-seat drivers, the boss more than the woman.

He looked outside again and shook his head incredulously. And they called London 'the Smoke'!

But where *was* the boss? According to Harlow, he was supposed to be dancing up and down on what passed for the runway, glaring at his watch and threatening to dock an honest pilot's pay an hour for every minute he was late – quite as though Unions had never been invented.

Carson had always suspected Harlow of being a romantic in the Victorian tradition. There was nothing out there except silence . . . and the fog.

Carson went back to his seat and switched off the motor; it looked like he was in for a wait. The rotors idled to a gradual halt. The silence slowly impinged and threatened to become oppressive.

Should he get out and go up to the house? Always providing he could find it in this fog. No, it was safer to sit tight and let them come to him. At least they'd have an idea of the right direction to strike out in.

But what was keeping them? Harlow might have exaggerated a bit, but he had left no real doubt about the urgency of the situation. Paul Jarvis had to get back to London and had to get there fast.

So why wasn't he here ready to board? Carson frowned, trying to peer through the murk. Visibility seemed to be about two feet. Only faintly-glowing globes at intervals gave him ammunition to fight off the doubt suddenly assailing him.

He *had* landed in the right place, hadn't he? It was unfamiliar territory down here and there must be more than one big estate, even complete with swimming pool and tennis court.

But surely not more than one would have all the lights turned on, in readiness for an arrival from the sky? No, everything was prepared here for his arrival – except the bloody passengers.

Ought he to get out and go looking for them? Was it expected that he should report to the big house, like a taxi-driver picking up a fare? Harlow had been most insistent upon the necessity for speed, but completely vague about what would happen once he had set the helicopter down in the grounds of the mansion. Perhaps even Harlow's romantic imagination was unable to proceed beyond that climax.

Carson tried to fight down his impatience. If he left the helicopter and went wandering around, he could easily become lost in this fog. It was so dense as to make it highly problematical that he could find Dower House itself, much less find his way back to an object so comparatively small as the helicopter. No, it was much better to stay put and let them find him.

But . . . where *were* they?

CHAPTER XX

Lillian stumbled crossing the lawn. She caught herself just short of falling and kept moving. She knew instinctively that the gun trained on her had not wavered. She knew also that there would be no use in arguing, pleading, or even tears. She had looked into the eyes of the man holding the gun and they had sent a chill through her that might never leave her. They were as cold, hard and unwavering as the gun he held. Dead eyes in a dead man. No use in attempting to appeal to any common humanity in him.

Who was he? Where had he come from? What did he want? He had said nothing after those first few words, just followed her relentlessly.

She veered slightly, but before the impulse to run could formulate itself completely, the gun prodded her in the back. He was too close for her to break away. In any case, where could she run? Not back to the house — he was blocking her way. It would be foolhardy to dart off into the fog, she would only get lost and it was quite possible that he would catch her before she could go far. In this fog, the terrain was as unfamiliar to her as it must be to him. Or was it unfamiliar to him?

The gun prodded her again and she moved forward. He seemed to know where they were going. Or was he guided, as she was, by the glow of light from the tennis court – growing stronger now – and the clatter of the helicopter's rotors?

Even as the thought crossed her mind, the clatter dwindled and died. The pilot must have killed the engines. The resulting silence was more unnerving than the constant noise had been.

'Keep moving!' The gun stabbed at her back again. Were those the only words he knew?

'Keep moving!'

Were there other sounds beyond them in the fog? A child whimpering? Were Paul and Genevieve, with Sandy, coming closer on a collision course with the gunman? If she were to scream and run now, would the warning be in time?

'All right.' In her concentration, she had not noticed that the ground under her feet had smoothed and hardened into the tennis court. Now a great awkward shape loomed ahead of them. Seen patchily through the swirling mist, it looked like some prehistoric monster insect waiting to devour them. One more nightmare image in this night of endless nightmare.

'Move!' The gun prodded her forward relentlessly. Despite the smooth asphalt surface, she stumbled, and threw out an arm to save herself from falling. Her hand connected with the cold metal surface of the helicopter. She knew then that it was too late.

'Right! Climb aboard,' he said. So he did know some other words, after all.

CHAPTER XXI

Carson's primary feeling was outrage. The incredulity came afterwards. Here he was, minding his own business, sitting in his own helicopter on an impromptu landing field waiting for his own boss on a private flight – and *this* had to happen! To him! On a night like this, when the fog alone was enough of a problem for any one man to have to face.

He, who had always prided himself on never getting involved. And here he was, involved up to his sodding ears!

'Please – ' the girl whispered. Had she noticed the tensing of his muscles, or merely sensed that he was about to try to tackle the man? 'Please don't. You're the only one who can fly this thing. We've got to get to London tonight.'

'She's right.' The gunman's voice was harsh, almost rusty from disuse, or the fog. 'Be sensible and nobody will get hurt.'

Carson forced himself to relax – or to seem to relax. 'What's up?' He twitched the corners of his mouth, it probably wasn't much of a smile, but it showed willing. He hoped. 'Harlow told me it was an emergency, but he didn't mention anything like this.'

'Harlow . . .' the girl breathed. It was as though she had been reminded of another, better world.

'He's waiting for us at the other end,' Carson said, since the name had seemed to encourage her. Who would have thought old Harlow could have had an effect like that on anyone? Especially on such an attractive female.

Perhaps it wasn't true, then, what they were saying about her and Paul Jarvis. Yet she was down here on his estate and — come to that — where *was* the boss? And who was this man holding a gun on him? What was going on here? The woman — Duxworthy, that was her name, Lillian Duxworthy — seemed as confused as he himself.

'What happened?' Carson spoke to her across the gunman, in a conversational tone, trying to keep the situation cool. 'Who is this man?'

'I don't know.' Lillian took a deep breath and went on unsteadily. 'He . . . he just appeared behind me . . . with that gun . . . as I was locking the front door. I think he'd been hiding in the cellar.'

'Never mind who I am,' the gunman ordered. He pushed Lillian forward, crowding them both together in the front of the cockpit. 'Just get this thing into the air!'

'You can't!' Lillian protested. 'Paul's coming — '

'Paul *was* coming,' the gunman mocked her. He turned to Carson and levelled the gun. 'Take it up!'

Involved up to his sodding ears — and through no fault of his own. A not particularly misspent life flashed in front of Carson's eyes. National Service at eighteen, going on to become a career soldier. Over four thousand hours of helicopter experience logged, going on to become an instructor. An early, honourable retirement on a pension that might have kept him, with a spot of beachcombing — but no, he'd had to decide to opt for a commercial career. (Well, how else could you afford to keep flying these days at these prices?) A rolling stone he'd been – and proud of it. But now it looked as though he might have rolled too far. Through no fault of his own, in a job that had seemed so innocent as to be in danger of being downright boring, it looked as though he might have rolled too far to ever roll back again.

'I can't take her up like this – ' Carson looked around, playing for time. Whatever was going on, the less he let himself be crowded, the better. 'You'll have to see to the steps and shut the door first.'

'I'll go – ' Lillian began to move. Carson hoped she'd have sense enough to hurl herself out of the door and escape into the fog. The gunman would be easier to cope with if there weren't another hostage to worry about.

'Stay where you are!' The gunman grabbed her arm. Carson cursed himself for having turned off the engines. If they were still going, he could lift the Sikorsky and tilt it a bit –

There were voices outside. The helicopter rocked sharply as someone leaped aboard and a man's voice said, 'Now, pass her up to me. Careful – '

The gunman pushed Lillian into the co-pilot's seat and half-crouched beside her. He would not be immediately noticeable to anyone boarding the aircraft. Carson turned and a wave of the gun let him know that he had not been forgotten. There was nothing he could do at the moment. A dead pilot was no use to anyone.

'Paul's here!' Lillian sounded triumphant, as though the mere fact of his presence had changed everything, as though the gunman were already disarmed and made captive. Carson stared at the instrument panel glumly. Lillian had a lot to learn.

'Keep quiet!' the gunman snarled. A soft gasp from Lillian betrayed that he had twisted her arm to reinforce the command.

'Daddy –' There was a child's whimpering cry in the cabin behind them. 'Daddy, it hurts –'

'It won't hurt much longer, sweetheart.' Paul Jarvis's voice was warm, confident and reassuring. 'We're on our way now.' He spoke, obviously to another person. 'Tilt the arm up between the seats so that I can lay her down. That's it. See if you can fasten a safety-belt around her lying down, while I see to the door.'

'Who are they?' the gunman demanded softly, urgently, of Lillian. 'How many more are there out there?'

'No more,' Lillian said. 'They're all aboard now.'

'Who's piloting?' Paul Jarvis demanded, blinking against the brightness of the cabin after the dark outside.

'Carson, sir,' Carson called out, switching on the engines. The gunman still crouched silent and indecisive, almost as though letting events take care of themselves.

'Lillian?' Paul called. 'Are you aboard?'

'Yes, Paul.' Her voice was faint. Again the betraying gasp told that she had been forced into making the reply. 'I'm here.'

'Right, Carson!' There was the slide and slam of the door and Paul Jarvis unconsciously echoed the gunman's earlier command. 'Take it up!'

Before the gunman could decide whether this was now what he wanted or not, Carson set the machine in motion. The gunman was off-balance, rattled. Keep him that way.

Lurching slightly, the helicopter clawed its way into the sky.

'Keep this damn thing steady!' the gunman snapped.

'What's the problem?' Out of the corner of his eye, Carson saw the gunman stagger before he managed to brace himself against the co-pilot's seat. 'She's steady as a rock.'

The temptation was strong to hurl the machine around a bit and knock the gunman off his feet, but he would still be able to fire the gun. And in such a restricted space –

Apart from which, there was still the question Lillian hadn't answered: who *were* those people behind him in the cabin? One of them was a child – a sick child, from the sound of it. And the boss was back there? Who else? In the short briefing he had been given over the telephone before taking off, Harlow had only told him that he was to pick up the boss and his secretary and bring them back to town, landing on the rarely-used helicopter pad at the top of City headquarters. No one else had been mentioned. Who were all these other people?

The child whimpered again and then began crying in earnest, a low desperate wail that filled the whole helicopter and rose penetratingly over the clatter of the rotors.

'Lillian?' Paul called. 'Lillian, come back here and give us a hand, will you?'

'Stay here!' The gunman snarled as Lillian automatically tried to struggle out of the co-pilot's seat.

'Lillian?' Evidently the boss was accustomed to instant obedience. There was a sharp note in his voice. The fog was thinning now as they continued to gain altitude. Carson abandoned his concern with events inside the helicopter and concentrated on lifting it completely above the fog. Once he was able to achieve some visibility outside, he might feel better able to cope with whatever was happening inside.

'Lillian?' Carson was aware of a figure moving along the cabin behind him. He did not look round.

'Lillian – have you told Carson about the change in the flight plan we'll need?'

'Don't worry.' The harsh voice spoke suddenly. 'He knows.'

'What?' In a perverse way, Carson found that he was enjoying hearing someone else register the same sort of shock that he had felt. 'I thought you were the co-pilot. But you're not! Who the hell are you?'

'Never mind! I'm the man in charge – that's all you have to know. And remember.'

'Paul.' Like the others, Lillian raised her voice to carry over the noise of the rotors. But not very much. EngAm was testing some new acoustical engineering equipment on their Sikorsky. Carson had been favourably impressed on the trip down to Dartmoor – it looked like another triumph shaping up for Paul Jarvis and EngAm. The inventing engineer had been nearly as clever as claimed and, with the new uprush in interest in helicopters for short-hop inter-city flights, it looked as though the noise problem which had hitherto banned the aircraft from city centres was about to be licked. But what good would a quiet aircraft do him now? It looked as though Paul Jarvis's long winning streak was heading for an abrupt end.

'Paul – he's got a gun. He – he must have been hiding in the wine cellar. Paul, he's wearing a prison uniform – ' Lillian's voice broke off on a sharp cry of pain.

'An escapee!' Carson listened in admiration as Paul Jarvis revealed a vocabulary that would have done credit to many a man without his advantages. Who would have believed that smooth figurehead at the Boardroom table could let rip like that? There was obviously more to the boss than met the eye.

'Never mind that.' The gunman cut across the flow of invective. 'Just shut up and answer a few questions. Who are those people back there with you?'

'My wife.' The answer seemed wrenched from Paul Jarvis. 'My wife and my little girl. The child is ill – appendicitis. We've got to get her to a hospital – '

'Is that so?' The gunman ignored the plea, if plea it was. The boss had sounded as though he thought he was still in command.

'That's so.' Paul Jarvis's voice was brisk. 'Carson, you'll have to contact London Air Traffic Control and file an emergency flight plan. We'll need to overfly London Control Zone and land in Coram's Fields, Bloomsbury, to set Sandy down for the Great Ormond Street Hospital. She needs an operation as soon as possible. Harlow is notifying them and they'll have an ambulance there waiting for her.'

Automatically, Carson reached out for the radio switch, momentarily forgetting their stowaway passenger in the urgency of the problem.

'Carson – don't bother!' The gunman's voice halted him. 'We're maintaining radio silence on this flight!'

Carson registered the news without surprise. It was hardly news. It bore out the feeling of doomed finality that had been wrapping itself around him like the blanket of fog outside. Gloomily, he added up the final tally of his list of unexpected and unwanted passengers: one short-tempered, high-powered employer; one gunman, an unknown quantity – as much as any escaped prisoner waving a gun around could be unknown; two women; and one child – a sick child, at that. *Fasten your safety-belts folks, we're in for a bumpy flight.*

'How long will it take us to reach London?' Ignoring the man with the gun, Paul Jarvis was still trying to prove that he was the boss.

'About an hour, maybe an hour and a half,' Carson answered carefully, trying to humour him without antagonizing the gunman. 'Depends how it goes.'

'Can't you make it any faster?'

'Well . . .' Carson temporized, waiting for the command that he knew must come next. 'Maybe it – '

'In fact,' the gunman interrupted, 'it's going to be slower than that. You'd better add a couple more hours on to that estimate.'

Carson waited, listening to the boss's choked-off exclamation of outrage. Paul Jarvis might be the man paying the piper, but he was no longer the man calling the tune.

'We're going to make a little detour first,' the gunman said. 'There's a place I have to get to – and you're going to drop me off there before you go on to London.'

The silence lengthened. The gunman was playing with them, enjoying his sense of power. Paul Jarvis disdained to ask the question; Carson knew that they would have to be told eventually and concentrated on flying the machine.

They broke through the final layer of fog. The air was cold and still up here, above them the crescent sliver of moon was cold and distant.

'The first stop is going to be Calais.'

CHAPTER XXII

Genevieve tried to be reasonable, and it was not reasonable to blame Lillian. It was irrational to suppose that Lillian had had any choice with the man holding a gun on her. Any more choice than Carson had now with the gun on him. But surely, *someone* could do something.

Sandy whimpered, although she could not know what was going on. She was only semi-conscious, but the pain must be gnawing at her again.

'We *must* go to London!' Genevieve burst out. 'Now! The child is ill! We must get her to a hospital at once!'

'Then the sooner you get me to Calais, the sooner you can turn round and get back to London.'

'We don't have enough fuel,' Carson said. It was worth a try.

'If there's enough fuel for London,' the gunman said, 'there's enough to take us across the Channel. You can refuel in France – *after* you've dropped me off.'

'I don't have charts for a Channel crossing,' Carson said. That, too, was worth a try, but he was beginning to realize that this customer wasn't going to be discouraged by trifles. Just how much was at stake?

'Then you'll just have to fly by the seat of your pants, won't you?' The gunman's voice was lazily amused. The more protests Carson made, the more amused he seemed to become. Somehow, it made him more sinister than threats or anger would have done. 'Just the way they used to do it in the old days.'

'No! You can't *do* this!' Genevieve struggled desperately with her seat-belt. If no one else would, she would hurl herself at this maniac and take the gun away from him! She would –

'Steady!' Paul hurried back to her, his hands caught hers and held them. 'Just take it easy. We'll come to some agreement.' He looked up at the gunman.

'Whoever you are,' he began bargaining, 'you must understand the child is dangerously ill. She needs immediate medical attention – '

'There are hospitals in France,' the gunman said. 'You can take her to one – *after* you've dropped me off.'

'We won't tell,' Lillian implored. 'We'll never tell anyone we've seen you. Just let us go to London first – and then the helicopter can carry you on to France.'

'You must need money – ' Paul reached for his wallet. The movement of the gun halted him. 'It's all right, I was only going to take out my wallet.' For a dangerous moment, contempt flashed. 'You don't imagine I carry a gun?'

'No,' the gunman said. 'I imagine you pay someone else to carry a gun for you. Just like you pay someone else to drive your car and fly your helicopter.' The contempt was mutual.

'Paul – ' This time it was Genevieve who captured his hands, willing him to relax. 'Be sensible.' Sandy had gone back to sleep, exhausted from the exertion of having been carried from Dower House Cottage to the helicopter, and it was as though her slumber had released Genevieve to think clearly again.

'Good advice,' the gunman approved. 'If everybody is sensible, nobody will get hurt. If not . . .' He let the thought die away.

'I'll pay you anything you want,' Paul Jarvis said.

'I don't need money,' the gunman said. 'All I need is the loan of your helicopter for a couple of hours – you're getting off cheap.' The man turned and Carson could feel the gun aiming at the back of his head. 'Are we heading for France?'

'We're on our way,' Carson said. He turned the Sikorsky towards the Channel.

Lillian gave a soft involuntary whimper.

'Not frightened, are you?' The gunman sounded genial. 'You'd better get back there with the others.' He stepped back, while Lillian lurched out of the co-pilot's seat and stumbled past him. 'And fasten your safety-belts,' he ordered.

Carson heard the sharp click as Lillian obeyed orders. But her expression evidently still left something to be desired.

'There's nothing to worry about,' the gunman assured her. 'It's just a short jump across the Channel. Nothing to it. They've even flown the Atlantic in a helicopter.'

'They had to refuel in flight nine times along the way,' Carson said sourly. 'And we don't carry an in-flight refuelling probe – even if anyone knew where to find us.' They carried flotation equipment, although it would be better if the gunman didn't know that. He seemed to know enough – but it was the sort of little learning that was a dangerous thing. What if he took it into his head to order them across the Atlantic? It didn't bear thinking about.

The gunman gave a short, sharp laugh, as though he had scored a point in some obscure game of his own.

The passengers — the hostages — seemed to be settled down for the moment, lost in a brooding recognition of their own plight. Carson hoped that they were capable of a realistic appraisal of the situation. Heroics were out. Helicopters weren't designed for aerobatic manoeuvres. They might not seem so perilous, chugging through the sky within comfortable sight of the ground — fog permitting — but let the engines fail and they plummeted to earth like a stone. And you were just as dead falling from 2000 feet as from 20,000 feet.

'Stop messing about with those controls!' The gunman ordered abruptly. So he wasn't as relaxed as he appeared on the surface. 'Keep still — and keep those hands where I can see what you're doing!'

'This isn't an airplane,' Carson said. 'There's more to it than that. I may not have so many instruments, but I have four main controls and I have to keep co-ordinating them at all times. If I stop messing about, we go down.'

There was silence while the gunman assimilated this. Carson hoped the passengers were assimilating it, too. The rotors spun on, filling the void with a companionable clatter. It was a great improvement on the helicopter noise the noise abatement societies complained about, it would be a pity if the experiment were to come to nothing. If the Sikorsky crashed, and all the experimental equipment with it, chances were that the experimental equipment would be blamed.

'If it's that tricky,' the gunman asked suspiciously, 'how come you're flying it alone? Why haven't you got a co-pilot?'

'I couldn't get hold of him tonight,' Carson said. 'This was an unscheduled flight and he was off on a heavy week-end. I didn't think he was really necessary – just to hop down here and back to London again.' His throat tightened with what, in other circumstances, might have been a sardonic laugh. 'It was just a milk run.'

There was an answering snort of amusement from the gunman. He could afford to laugh – things were going his way. 'That's pretty good, Carson,' he said. 'Pretty good.'

'You have the advantage – ' Carson decided to chance his luck while the gunman seemed to be in a better mood. All the psychologists interviewed during and after other hi-jackings invariably recommended that the hostages try to make some contact with their captor – and the boss and his harem seemed to be out of action for the moment, still reeling from shock. It was up to him.

'You have the advantage – ' Carson said. 'In more ways than one.' Sure enough, the gunman gave a complacent chuckle at the feeble joke. 'You know my name. How about telling me yours? Or – ' he added cautiously – 'something we can call you, if you don't want us to know your real name.'

'I don't mind telling you my real name,' the gunman said. 'I'm Slade.'

'Slade.' Carson felt a cold chill travel down his back, without immediately realizing why. After a moment, the name clicked into place and his spine became a column of solid ice. 'Slade the Blade.'

'That's what the newspapers called me.' Slade
sounded gratified at the instant recognition. Perhaps
he'd thought he'd been forgotten in the years since they
had put him away. But it would take longer than that
before the public forgot Slade.

Slade the Blade ... Paul met Lillian's eyes, both of them
beginning to realize the full extent of their plight.
Genevieve, occupied with fretting over Sandy's pulse,
paid no attention. The name meant nothing to her. She
had been in Canada at the time of the Old Bailey trial
and, while the case had been a minor sensation in
England, other countries had had their own sensational
cases and murder happening so far away was either
not reported at all, or else relegated to truncated reports
in the inner pages of their newspapers. At that time, the
activities of the French Liberationists in Quebec would
have been taking up Canadian headlines.

Slade the Blade ... He'd left a trail of blood across
London and the South-East, with occasional forays into
the rival gang territory of Birmingham. He'd started
small, with non-fatal stabbings and carried on with
increasing intensity until he had left three women
slashed to ribbons before he had been caught.

The biggest question had been whether he'd be sent
to Dartmoor or Broadmoor. Even his own gang
members were afraid of him. There was something not
quite *right* about him, they'd admitted under oath and
still squirming nervously under his baleful gaze from
the dock. The decision had been in favour of Dartmoor
when it was eventually revealed that the women had all
been on the fringes of gangdom and had been used as

decoys in various bank raids. The judge and jury had assumed that, with a sound motive for killing the women, the accused might not be so crazy as he might wish to appear, despite the unnecessary savagery of the murders. But always there had remained that lingering doubt in the minds of the general public: should the decision really have been for Broadmoor? The judge had sentenced Slade to life imprisonment with the recommendation that the prisoner should serve a period of not less than thirty years.

But now Slade had escaped from Dartmoor and was here in ominous command of the executive helicopter – and with three females in his haul of hostages.

'I still have my blade,' Slade said softly. 'Do you want to see it?'

'No thanks,' Carson said. 'The gun scares me quite enough.'

Slade chuckled. 'That's the right attitude. You just keep thinking like that and no one's going to get hurt.'

If you could trust his promises. And why had he been so willing to reveal his name? Because he was thirsting for the recognition and fear it would bring? Or because it did not matter if they knew who he was or where he was going? Because he intended to kill them all before he disembarked from the helicopter?

'Please, Mr Slade,' Genevieve said carefully, 'you must understand my child is very ill.' Her caution was the natural caution of anyone faced with a threatening gun. She alone among the adults had no idea of the real extent of the threat, of the sort of mind they might be dealing with. 'As a mother, I ask you, I beg of you – let us get this child to a hospital.'

It was worth a try, Carson supposed. And, fortunately she'd worded it in a way to appeal to Slade's lust for power. It wouldn't work, but it wouldn't antagonize him, either.

'The kid looks all right to me,' Slade said.

'It's appendicitis,' Genevieve said. 'I know. I was a nurse . . . once. She's quiet now because she's exhausted. The attack has been severe. If the appendix ruptures, peritonitis can set in so quickly – ' Genevieve's voice broke.

'So what?' Slade shrugged. 'What's one brat more or less? The world is over-populated already.'

Genevieve caught them unprepared. They had not noticed that she had quietly undone her seat-belt. At Slade's words, she threw herself forward with a scream – a tigress fighting for her cub.

'I'll kill you!' She hurled herself at Slade, clawing for his eyes. The attack nearly succeeded because of its suddenness and because it had come from such an unlikely quarter. Genevieve had appeared least concerned about what was happening, worried only about her child. Perhaps that was why Slade had been baiting her.

With an answering snarl, Slade fended her off with his free hand while the other hand brought up the gun and smashed it across her temple.

Genevieve fell back and slumped to the floor.

'Don't move!' Slade ordered the others. Genevieve could not move; she was unconscious. He glanced down at her, as though contemplating a pistol whipping.

'Leave her alone,' Paul said roughly. 'It was your own fault. What did you expect when you spoke to her like that? She's French-Canadian. She has a temper.'

'Not like your little English rose, eh?' Slade looked at Lillian, who sat frozen in horror, mostly because they had lost such a golden opportunity. If only they'd had any warning of what Genevieve had intended, they could all have acted together and overpowered him. In that first startled instant of attack, he had been completely vulnerable.

And they, as unprepared as he, had lost their chance.

'Stay where you are!' Paul had incautiously started to move.

'I just want to pick her up,' Paul said tightly. 'You can't leave her lying there.' He swallowed. 'Let me put her back in her seat.'

'You haven't got the message yet,' Slade said. 'I can do anything I want to do. It's her own fault she's on the floor. Let her stay there.'

The surge of fury surprised Paul. It had been a long time since he had felt so fiercely about anything. Even when Harlow had told him of the impending treachery of his high-echelon colleagues – men he had trusted and in many cases, raised to the position they now held – he had not felt such molten fury flooding his veins. There had been a cold deadly anger, but nothing like this. This was the completely primitive reaction of a caveman seeing his woman struck down by an enemy.

One of his women. But the familiar guilt was no longer operating, it had been swamped by fury. Yes, one of his women. One of the three hostages to fortune he had accumulated along the way. Hostages now preempted by the mad gunman aboard his own helicopter.

Genevieve had been right, Paul realized. Slade would have to be killed. If not, he would kill them all. It was as simple as that. He must kill Slade. Moreover, he *wanted* to kill him. It was another atavistic impulse, recognizably higher on the evolutionary scale: the Middle Ages, perhaps. In no other way would the stain on his honour be avenged.

'Mummy.' Sandy stirred and whimpered. 'Mummy...

Genevieve moaned as though in answer, her child's voice reaching her through the layers of unconsciousness. She turned her head slightly. A dark bruise was already discolouring her temple.

'Mummy . . .' Sandy called. 'Where *are* you?'

'Mummy's resting,' Paul said. 'Go back to sleep, there's a good girl. It's all right. Daddy's here.'

Slade gave a snort of laughter. Paul did not trust himself to speak again. His voice might give him away. He must bide his time and not let Slade suspect the craving for vengence he had roused.

'Mummy . . .' Sandy was regaining consciousness. She would not be soothed. 'Mummy . . .'

'Shut up!' Slade snapped at the fretful child.

'Let me go to her,' Lillian appealed to Slade. 'She'll be all right if someone sits by her. Please, let me go to her. I – I won't try anything –'

'That's right,' Slade looked at her, almost genially. 'You won't, will you? You and I know each other already, don't we, blondie? All right, you can go to her. I'll trust you not to try anything. You haven't got the guts.'

For that, Lillian decided quietly, she would kill him.

CHAPTER XXIII

The helicopter chugged through the night sky with its cargo of hatred.

Carson risked turning his head again. He was doing this more frequently now, getting Slade used to it, careful not to meet any eyes or seem to be giving any signals, just keeping an eye on the situation in the cabin behind him.

And thinking furiously. Despite the gun, the pilot was still the man in real command. As long as they were up in the air.

There were tricks you could do with a helicopter. Military display teams showed off some very flashy ones. Not the least of which was somersaulting the helicopter in one swift manoeuvre. That would really send Slade flying. The trouble was, it would also send everyone else flying, too. And, with a sick kid, it just wasn't on.

There was also the slight matter of the equipment he had at his fingertips. The display teams were flying light, trim craft, without an ounce of superfluous weight and not carrying any passengers. They weren't hamstrung by a cow of a commercial craft — politely designated as 'medium weight', but actually carrying extra weight for the acoustical modulation they were testing. Not to mention all the modifications a multi-national corporation on an ego trip could conceive and the Civil Air Authority could be persuaded to approve.

Ordinarily, it wouldn't have mattered. He'd been ferrying EngAm executives all over Great Britain and the Continent for two years now without giving the aerobatic limitations of the aircraft a second thought. Who would ever have thought that such a thing could suddenly become crucial?

Be honest, Carson — with yourself, if nobody else. There was one other consideration. If he started to get too tricky, there was no guarantee that Slade would wait to ask questions before he began shooting. And that old, jocular reassurance to nervous passengers still held true.

The pilot wants to live, too.

'Where am I?'

Genevieve, with one part of her mind, heard her own question with incredulity. She had heard it from so many patients and wondered at it. She wondered no longer. It was no surprise that people should ask that.

Where was she?

She was on a flat, hard, vibrating surface. When she opened her eyes, all she could see were legs: chair-type legs; human legs; a close-up view of nuts and bolts and, incongruously, shoes. Her head ached savagely and there was a throbbing, hurtful roaring in her ears.

'Where am I?' She raised a hand to her aching forehead and struggled up on one elbow, trying to focus properly.

'Stay right where you are!'

The sharp command halted her efforts to rise. She froze, groggily propped up on one elbow, groping for a memory to sort out the situation, to tell her where she was and what was happening to her.

Nothing came. Nothing except a sense of danger and an instinct to lie low and pretend to be worse than she was.

She groaned and slumped back on to the floor, buying time in which to assess her predicament.

'Please – ' another voice pleaded. 'Please let me help her.' A female voice – an enemy voice.

Mais non! A correction arose from deep within her consciousness. The whole pattern had subtly shifted, changed. This was no longer an enemy. Things were no longer what they had been.

What was happening? She lay still, listening.

'It's all right,' a warm masculine voice said reassuringly. 'Take it easy, Genevieve. It's going to be all right.'

'Paul . . .' she sighed, leaning back against the reassuring arm.

But there was something wrong.

The voice had been Paul's, but the arm was not.

The arm was smaller, softer . . . female. The arm belonged to the enemy.

Non! The automatic correction came from deep within her again. No longer the enemy. There was a worse enemy now – a more malignant fate which threatened them all. This was an ally. Genevieve opened her eyes, then closed them again, fighting for remembrance.

'Mummy . . . ?' The childish voice rose in a penetrating shriek. *'Mum-mee . . .'*

'Alexandra!' Genevieve fought against the encircling arms. 'Sandy!' Friendly arms, she realized belatedly. Arms restraining her from abrupt movement, arms trying to protect her from the consequences

of her own instincts. Those arms had once belonged to
an enemy – yesterday's adversary.

Today the world had turned, tilted abruptly. Today
there was a newer, more dangerous enemy. An enemy
who would steal life itself – not only one's own, but the
life of one's child –

'Sandy!' she cried again, still befogged, still fighting
for some basis of recognition in this menacing world.
'Paul . . .' And, once more, despairingly, 'Sandy!'

How had the world changed so swiftly and so much
for the worse? She fought against the restraining arms,
even knowing them to be friendly.

'Sandy!'

They were moving too quickly. If they kept moving at
this pace, they would soon be out over the Channel.
Once they left the shoreline of England behind, their
chances of survival diminished with every mile. If
they actually reached France and had to set down –

They needed more time. Time to adjust to the
situation. Time to think. Carson glanced over his
shoulder, registering that everyone's attention was
concentrated on Genevieve.

There was one way to buy time. If he could get
away with it.

Carson adjusted the controls as inconspicuously as
possible. Would Slade notice the change in pitch, the
loss of forward movement? He checked back over his
shoulder. Slade seemed to be lost in plans of his own;
he was quiet, inward-looking, but still not missing anything that was going on around him.

'What are you doing?' Slade demanded sharply.

'Can't you keep your hands off those controls for ten seconds?'

'No, I can't. I keep telling you – ' Carson let exaggerated patience seep into his voice. 'This isn't a fixed-wing aircraft. You have to keep adjusting the rotors constantly, and the pitch and the – '

'Carson is the best pilot EngAm has,' Paul Jarvis intervened, his voice charged with a meaning he hoped only Carson would pick up. 'Leave him alone. He knows what he's doing.'

And so do I. The controls only needed constant adjusting when the craft was actually hovering. *Good man, Carson.* He was using delaying action to gain time. But could he gain enough time? And how much good would it do them?

How long would it be before Harlow realized they were not coming and reported them missing? Longer than it would have been under normal circumstances, certainly, because Harlow knew that they would be landing to get Sandy to the hospital. He would allow them anything from half an hour upwards for that – perhaps longer, if the possible complications had set in and Paul might have gone to the hospital with her. Even the lack of a telephone call would not unsettle him unduly. It would take any length of time before he realized something was seriously wrong and sent out an alarm.

Even then, how much good would it do? Granted that EngAm would immediately institute a full-scale air-sea search – which was by no means certain if the Extraordinary General Meeting carried on as had been planned – could they be found? Or would they already

be over French territory by then? It was a good ploy,
but Carson could not hover indefinitely. Already Slade
seemed to be growing restive, as though suspecting
trouble.

And even supposing that the search planes caught
up with them while they were still over English
territory, what then? They would still be cooped up in a
helicopter with an escaped convict holding a gun on
them. Could the rescuing planes actually force the helicopter to earth? Unlikely. Could they do anything
except fly alongside and monitor events from the
outside? It would still be a hostage situation.

There was one other aspect Paul did not care to
contemplate: would they be reported missing at all?
How dependable was Harlow when it came to the
crunch?

Harlow was weak and had an eye to the main chance.
One knew that and made allowances. To the limit of
his ability, Harlow was loyal. Unfortunately, Harlow
had a limited ability.

In order to report the helicopter missing, Harlow
would have to admit that he had dispatched it in the
first place – and for what purpose. Which would mean
admitting to his new masters that he had been plotting
against them, throwing in his lot with the old regime, a
regime which even now might be lying in a heap of
smouldering rubble somewhere in the English country-
side.

And they would be his new masters. Without Paul
Jarvis present in person, the meeting would achieve
the aims the Board intended. He would be deposed,
with control effectively wrenched away from him. The
company he had built up would be run by men less

competent and less talented, but infinitely more skilled in the art of manipulation.

Harlow could never be expected to stand up to them and confess that he had known all along that Paul Jarvis was still in England instead of Canada and he had not let them know it. Nor could he admit that he had betrayed them to Paul and conspired to bring Paul back to London in time to ruin their plans for the meeting.

No, Harlow could not be depended upon for any help. Harlow would lie low and hope for the best. And, for Harlow, the best might be that pile of smoking wreckage with no survivors. He could then plead ignorance of the whole thing and it would be assumed that Paul had been acting on his own.

'What the hell is happening?' Slade demanded. 'We're not moving! What are you trying to pull?'

'Nothing.' Carson sent the helicopter slipping sideways. 'We've run into turbulence. That's all. Can't you feel it?' He went down a few feet, came up again and sent the machine backwards briefly. 'The air currents are fighting us. But there's nothing to worry about.'

'There better not be!' But the bluster was meaningless. Even Slade knew that he could do nothing about the weather. As long as he didn't suspect it wasn't the weather, they were a short step ahead of him.

'I ought to radio in for weather information,' Carson said worriedly. 'We don't know what we may be heading into. The meteorological picture is changing.'

'We keep radio silence!' Slade snapped.

'But — ' Carson made a pretence of protesting, although he was limp with relief. There had been only the slightest chance that Slade might have called his bluff and allowed him to get a weather forecast. Then the fat would have been in the fire.

'Radio silence!' Slade reiterated. 'What kind of fool do you think I am?'

'You're in charge,' Carson admitted, sending the helicopter into a gentle bucking motion.

'Mum-mee –' The child's voice rose shrilly behind him. 'It hurts –'

Christ! He'd forgotten all about the kid! Carson steadied the helicopter guiltily.

'Sorry, everyone,' he called back over his shoulder. 'I'll try to keep it steady.' It was the best he could do by way of apology without giving the game away.

'That's all right,' Paul answered with understanding. 'Just do the best you can.'

CHAPTER XXIV

'Isn't there anything we can do for her?' Lillian asked Genevieve. 'A hot drink?' She gestured towards the basket she had brought aboard. How many centuries ago had she packed it? 'I have some coffee –'

'Not coffee,' Genevieve vetoed quickly. 'It will wake her up. It would be better if she went back to sleep.'

'Coffee?' Slade asked with interest. It was to his advantage to keep awake. 'I wouldn't mind some of that.'

'A sweet, perhaps?' Lillian reached for her handbag. 'I have some peppermints.'

'They won't help her.' Genevieve shrugged. 'But perhaps they might distract her.' Automatically she continued smoothing Sandy's brow, her head lowered in case her sudden thought might show in her face. Lillian's handbag had reminded her – in her own handbag, she had a small phial of sleeping pills. It might be as well to give one to Sandy, but it might be even better if all of them could be poured into M'sieu Slade. He had said that he wanted coffee . . .

Lillian marked the furtive half-turn of Genevieve's body as she twisted to conceal the movement of her hand sliding towards her handbag. Her other hand continued stroking the child's brow, slightly more ostentatiously now, as though drawing attention away from what she was really doing.

Interesting, Lillian thought, watching the handbag glide inch by inch along the floor and disappear behind the concealing folds of Genevieve's skirt.

With one eye on Slade, Lillian rummaged in her own handbag for the peppermints, at the same time quietly palming the metal nail file she had bought on the last business trip to New York. It had a point – blunted, unfortunately, for nail cleaning. But it was strong – metal coated with diamond dust, carrying a lifetime guarantee. 'We can do better than diamond dust,' Paul had laughed at her. Later that enchanted afternoon they had gone to Cartier's and chosen an engagement ring. The ring was in the office safe now because it had not seemed tactful to wear it this week-end, but she always carried the nail file as a sort of lucky talisman.

'Here we are.' Lillian snapped the handbag shut and held out the tube of peppermints to Genevieve. While attention was focused on that action, she quietly slipped the nail file into the pocket of her skirt. It might not be much of a weapon, but it was better than nothing.

'*Merci.*' Genevieve accepted the tube of peppermints not quite quickly enough to hide the fact that she already held another tube in her hand.

Their glances crossed, met, and slid away.

Slade watched them curiously. 'Very polite,' he said. 'Just one big happy family, are we?' He looked at Paul with open speculation.

'We try to be civilized,' Paul said expressionlessly.

Three decent people caught in a trap. Lillian remembered her original summation of their situation and could have wept for her own *naïveté. Three people who didn't know the meaning of the word 'trap'. Until now.*

'M'sieu Slade would like some coffee.' Genevieve spoke softly to Lillian. 'Would you pass the Thermos, please?'

Lillian met Genevieve's dark eyes a fraction of a second before the lashes lowered and neatly caught the dangerous message in them.

'Yes, why not?' Lillian passed the Thermos across to Genevieve and pulled the basket forward. 'How about sandwiches?' she queried generally, providing a further distraction which allowed Genevieve to turn away while opening the Thermos and pouring the coffee.

'Very civilized, indeed,' Slade approved. 'You've got your women well trained, mister.'

'A chicken sandwich — ' Lillian thrust it at Paul quickly, seeking to quell the fury that erupted in his face. It would do no good for Paul to launch himself at the gunman in an all-out attack. Genevieve had tried that — and failed. Furthermore, whereas Slade had merely struck Genevieve with the gun, he might actually pull the trigger on another male.

'I'll take that!' Slade stretched out the hand not holding the gun, conscious of a roaring hunger despite the food he had stolen in the house. Was it nerves? Or was it the taste of non-prison food, something not mass-produced and tiresomely bland and predictable? He didn't know. He only knew that he felt as though he might never again get enough food to assuage his constant hunger.

'Here you are – ' Lillian tossed it to him quickly before Paul could make any threatening move. Paul was even more furious now, but that couldn't be helped. Genevieve had to have time to attempt her plan. Whatever it might be.

Lillian instinctively felt that it would be safer if she was not too aware of what Genevieve was going to try. Just as she felt that it would be safer if Genevieve did not realize that she now had a sort of weapon – in the shape of the nail file – in her own pocket.

What neither of them was sure of, neither of them could inadvertently betray.

She was conscious that Genevieve seemed to be using more motions than the simple act of unscrewing the Thermos top and pouring coffee into it usually called for.

Lillian looked away hastily, lest Slade follow the direction of her gaze and notice what she had noticed.

'Where's that coffee?' Slade's voice was muffled. He had crammed half the sandwich into his mouth in one bite and was already looking towards the picnic basket for another. The man ate as though there were no tomorrow. Perhaps, for him, there wasn't – at least, not one he could be sure of.

'Coming.' Genevieve swirled the inch of coffee around the bottom off the cup. *Mon Dieu!* – would the filthy stuff never dissolve? If it did not, could he be persuaded that it was sugar thickening the dregs? Frantically, despairingly, she filled the cup nearly to the brim with coffee. 'How much sugar does M'sieu take?'

'Two spoonfuls.' Slade watched greedily as she spooned sugar into the cup. 'Don't be stingy with them.' He grinned. 'I need all the energy I can get.'

Was her hand shaking too much to carry the liquid to him? Genevieve took a deep breath and closed her eyes momentarily. She had never killed a man before. She had never met a man who deserved to die as much as this one did. She would do it and sleep the sleep of the just for the rest of her life, untroubled by guilt or nightmares. She had only one concern: was there enough powder in the coffee to kill him?

If not, was the solution strong enough to render him senseless so that the job could be finished in some other way?

For he must die. In the nightmare world her life had suddenly devolved into, that was the only certainty. He must die.

Unsteadily she rose to her feet, angry with herself at her own unsteadiness. There was no reason to be nervous about performing such a task. No more so than if one were to stamp upon a loathsome insect. Except that an insect would more probably be free of blame than the contemptible one who was watching her advance with such an ugly, knowing smirk on his face.

No, her only regret was that the manner of his going

would be so painless that he would be unaware of it. A
pity that she had not the means to send him to his knees
in shrieking agony before he died!

She had not known that she could hate so much. But
then, no one had ever threatened her child before.

A fresh moan from Sandy in the background
strengthened her resolve and curved her lips in a smile
as she offered Slade the cup.

'*Bon appétit, M'sieu,*' she murmured.

Carson caught the false note in her voice. Without
knowing what, he knew it boded ill to someone – to
Slade. Moving casually, secretly, he turned to look over
his shoulder.

'That's right.' Slade responded to Genevieve's faint
smile. 'Feeling more friendly now, aren't you? Just
stay like that and we won't have any problems.' He
raised the plastic cup in salute to her. 'Your health – '

Abruptly, Carson knew what she had done. And it
wouldn't work. Slade would feel himself going – and
there were enough bullets in that Magnum to account
for all of them before he slipped into unconsciousness.

And he would. Slade was not a man to give way
without a fight – without taking as much revenge as he
could exact. Slade was crazy enough already. As he
saw the prospect of freedom blurring and slipping
away, he would go completely wild. There would be a
massacre within the narrow confines of the aircraft –
and they would all perish.

But it had been a good try. You had to give the lady
top marks for trying. Too bad it had never had a
chance of working.

With a silent, regretful sigh, Carson tilted the

Sikorsky abruptly and dropped it six feet at the same time.

There was a raging curse from Slade – but it was better than a fusillade of bullets spraying the interior of the cabin.

'Sorry, folks – ' Carson glanced back over his shoulder, taking in the spreading brown stain on the carpeted floor, the fury in Slade's face and the lacklustre expression on the faces of the others.

Especially Genevieve. If Slade were to look at her now, the whole game would be given away.

'Turbulence!' Carson gestured with one hand, sideslipping the aircraft again, directing Slade's attention to the night sky outside. 'Can't be helped. It's pretty rough out there.'

'It looks all right to me,' Slade said suspiciously. He had obviously caught some of the psychic vibrations within the cabin but was unable to interpret them.

'That's the trouble with turbulence – ' Carson took the helicopter up ten feet and dropped it again abruptly – 'you can't see it. You can only feel it.'

'Yeah?' Slade squinted through the Plexiglass casing. The fog was thinning and there were glimpses of the earth beneath them. 'Well, hold it steady, can't you?'

'Doing my best,' Carson said cheerfully. He rocked the craft from side to side. 'I don't like it any better than you do. I've got to keep this thing in the air, after all.'

Genevieve had been hurled back against her seat by the abrupt drop of the aircraft. She slumped there now, indifferent to the racketing about of the craft and to the fresh moans from Sandy. Her mesmerized gaze was riveted on the brown stain spreading out from the orange Thermos cup on the cabin floor. She looked as though she might burst into tears.

Slade turned his attention back to the occupants of the cabin, looking from one to the other questingly, as though scenting some danger he had not identified. His gaze returned to the brown stain on the floor.

'Actually, there's a bar at the back – ' Lillian distracted him quickly. 'Perhaps you'd rather have a proper drink instead – '

'That's more like it.' Slade glanced at her with approval. 'The others have been holding out on me, have they? That wasn't very friendly. I'll have a double Scotch – but don't get any ideas about getting me drunk.'

'I'm sure you can hold your liquor very well.' Conscious of Paul's pained disapproval, Lillian moved to the rear of the compartment and slid down the hatch concealing the bar. She poured Slade's drink.

'Anyone else?' Automatically, she fell into the accustomed hostess role.

'Nobody else!' Slade spoke decisively. 'Just me. We don't want a lot of drunken passengers reeling around maybe thinking they ought to try to be heroes, do we?' He laughed harshly.

There was a corkscrew for the wine bottles in the rack behind the bar. A corkscrew with a sharp glittering point. Could you stab with a corkscrew? Perhaps not, but you could certainly rip open skin.

Under cover of closing and securing the bar hatch again, Lillian took the corkscrew and transferred it into her pocket with the nail file.

Carrying the drink carefully, she made her way

down the aisle to Slade, conscious that he was covering her with the gun at every step. Perhaps he expected her to spring at him or to hurl the drink in his face.

She handed it to him slowly and returned to her seat. He looked at her uncertainly, as though suspecting she had just put something over on him, but not sure what.

Slade was many things, but he was not a fool. It might be safer for them all had he been.

'There goes the meeting, I'm afraid.' Lillian broke the silence, looking at her watch, then at Paul, then back at her watch, staring down at it as though the hands were conveying some message. Something about the point of no return. She frowned accusingly at the watch face, as though that alone were responsible for the cold sinking feeling in the pit of her stomach. Soon, someone was going to have to do something, or it would be too late.

'I suppose so.' Paul did not sound unduly concerned. He, too, was now alert to the reality of the situation in which they found themselves. The loss of a company could not possibly compare with the loss of all their lives.

'What will you do?' The question presupposed that they would get out of this alive. That there would be a future in which something could be done to retrieve the loss.

But they had to play it that way. Slade was giving them his full attention now as he sipped his drink — attention which must be kept away from the puddle of milky brown liquid until it dried up and neutralized its deadly secret. He must not suspect that they had so far abandoned hope as to begin to mobilize against him.

'Do?' Unexpectedly, Paul raised his arms slowly and stretched luxuriously. Had he realized what had happened, or was it an accident that he had moved to catch and hold Slade's nervous stare?

'Do?' His lazy, heart-breaking grin spread across his face. 'I suppose I'll just have to start all over again. What else is there to do?'

'Ah, yes.' Genevieve came back to life. She turned her head to gaze solemnly at Paul. 'Yes, men always like starting again, don't they, and doing the same thing over and over? Like some dog which learns one trick and expects to be praised just for repeating it again and again. Sometimes on command – and sometimes just to earn the praise he knows it will bring.'

'Genevieve – ' Paul leaned forward with concern. There was a strange look on her face. Was she cracking under the strain? 'Genevieve . . .' He hesitated. 'Are you all right?'

'Yes, yes.' She looked at him blankly, her eyes unseeing – or seeing something beyond them all. 'Of course I'm all right. Why should you doubt it? Because I speak the truth? You're no longer used to that, are you, Paul? How many years has it been since anyone has dared to speak the truth to you? You've become far too important these days. People only tell you what they think you want to hear.'

'She's got your number all right, mister.' Slade was grinning openly, enjoying the scene. 'This one isn't as tame as you thought she was. The party's getting rough.'

'Genevieve, for God's sake – ' Paul was unnerved.

Genevieve had taken everything so well and now to crack up at a time like this and start talking – 'Not in public!'

'*Pas devant les domestiques.* Is that it, Paul?' Genevieve gave a high, mirthless laugh.

The helicopter tilted sharply and the orange plastic Thermos cup rolled across the floor to lodge by Paul's foot. He picked it up automatically and glanced down at it, at first casually and then stiffening with apprehension. That strange powdery sludge at the bottom of the cup bore no resemblance to the normal sugary residue. Abruptly, he knew what Genevieve had just attempted – and why her failure was leading her across the borders of hysteria.

Conscious of Slade's curious gaze, he forced himself to relax and look away from the cup. In doing so, he met Lillian's eyes and realized that she, too, knew what Genevieve had been up to. More, that she had known – or suspected – all along. That was why she had moved so quickly to divert Slade with the whisky.

Lillian looked away. Inadvertently, she encountered Genevieve's mordant gaze and shrank back as Genevieve began speaking again.

'*Oui*, Paul. You will enjoy starting again. A new wife, a new company – the very struggle is the breath of life to you, isn't it? Perhaps if you had had a harder time with the company, you would not have been so ready to begin again with another woman – '

The devil of it was that there might just be a grain of truth in her assessment of the situation, Paul admitted to himself. If things had not been so easy – so boring, after a while – he might not . . . he just might not . . . have looked around for new fields to conquer. He was uncomfortably aware that Lillian was watching him with speculation in her eyes and he avoided looking at her. He did not want to meet Genevieve's eyes, either. He continued staring into the depths of the plastic Thermos cup until he realized that too much attention paid to it might draw Slade's attention – and that could be fatal.

Paul risked a glance in Slade's direction. Yes, fatal. Already Slade's amusement at the scene before him was fading, a frown shadowing his forehead.

'You will build it all up again, Paul,' Genevieve went on. 'And in time, when the new company is big enough, no doubt you will wish to have a new family with your new wife. Perhaps this time you will have a son. You'd like that, Paul, wouldn't you? A son to take over the business from you? And so, you would work harder than ever – but your wife would have to stay at home to look after the child. And then, Paul, that would mean a new secretary – ' She glanced at Lillian slyly, a catlike smile curving her lips. Lillian was busy pretending not to notice, not to listen, but her mouth quivered involuntarily.

'That's enough, Genevieve,' Paul said soothingly. He slipped the plastic cup behind him on the seat, trying to push it down between the cushions, so that Slade might never know what had so nearly happened.

'A new secretary, Paul,' Genevieve's voice insinuated 'And then you could start over yet again . . . '

The helicopter bucked and dropped, then climbed again. It was a mistake. It bought Slade back to full consciousness of his present surrounding, no longer amused by the warfare between the two women.

'Hold this damned thing steady!' he barked at Carson.

'I'm trying,' Carson said patiently, sensing that Slade's temper was on an ever-shortening leash. He dismissed the idea of adding anything more, either in explanation or apology. Slade's patience was wearing too thin.

'Where are we?' Slade squinted through the Plexiglass of the cockpit. 'Why can't we see water yet? Why are we still over land? What are you trying to pull?'

'We're just tossed a bit off course by the weather —' Carson spoke quickly, his ears catching the click as Slade took the safety-catch off his gun. 'Not far off,' he added hastily. 'If I could just radio for a —'

'No radio! If I have to say it again, I'll smash the sodding thing! You're lucky I haven't already.' Slade was trying to keep cool, to lull them into a false sense of security. 'I'm letting you keep it so that you can use it after you've dropped me and get your clearances for a proper landing.'

'Thank you,' Carson said dryly, trying to sound as though he might actually believe that Slade was going to let them survive. Slade didn't want to smash the radio because an eventual examination of the wreckage would reveal that fact and start the police and aviation officials figuring things out. 'You're very kind.'

'I'm not so bad, once you get to know me,' Slade said ingratiatingly. 'But if I don't see water down below pretty soon, I'm going to blow your head off.'

'Less than ten minutes now,' Carson promised. 'Don't worry. You'll see all the water you want.'

CHAPTER XXV

Carson headed straight for the Channel. There was nothing more to be gained by stalling around over land – they would be better off over the water. Even without the flotation equipment they carried, the Sikorsky, with its boat-shaped fuselage, could set right down in the water. That was why NASA had used it to retrieve astronauts from space capsules after splashdown. They would be safer over water, if Slade should go berserk then –

Carson shuddered at the closeness of the escape. But did Genevieve realize that the coffee had not been spilled accidentally? When she discovered it, would she forgive him?

Why should he care? He shook himself mentally. If they got out of this at all, they would have used up a lifetime's aggregate luck. Such minor niceties as hurt feelings had no place in anyone's considerations at this juncture.

Genevieve had had the right idea – she had just gone about it in the wrong way. Slade must be got rid of. But what was the right way to do it?

Carson looked back over his shoulder. It was awfully silent back there after the burst of discord. It made him uneasy. Instinctively, he felt that Slade should not be allowed too much time to brood on his own thoughts. If at least one corner of Slade's mind could be kept distracted, they would all have a better chance.

If Slade could be thrown off-balance and kept off-balance, not given time to think a situation – an emergency – through, then there was a possibility that he might be stampeded into some hasty action that would rebound to their advantage.

Once they were over water, it might be simpler. Carson pushed the Sikorsky forward at a faster speed. He would slow down, he would hover again, once they were out over the Channel.

Slade was going to kill them anyway. No one could have any doubt about that. No one except the kid, who – drifting into and out of consciousness – had no realization of what was happening at all.

They were particularly vulnerable because they were in a helicopter and Slade had a gun. Not just a gun – a Magnum, which could stop a car engine block. One shot hitting the helicopter would blow it out of the sky. Slade held all the aces. Aces, hell – he held every available card in his hand!

And there was nothing they could do about it. The turbulence ploy was about played out. Slade was increasingly suspicious of every pitch and roll of the aircraft. Apart from which, the sky was clear, the moon shining bright, the few clouds in sight motionless and becalmed – even someone less credulous than Slade might smell a rat if the helicopter continued on an erratic course.

But what could be done about Slade? How could they get rid of him? Even if they disembarked him safely in France, there would certainly be a parting bullet sent through the rotor axis as they fought for altitude and safety, to send them crashing to earth with the inevitable explosion and fire. Slade would not leave any witnesses alive. Without their testimony, there was no one to reveal the method of his final escape, nor the country where the hunt for him should be started. Without a witness, Slade would be deemed to be on the run somewhere in England and the hunt for him would centre there. Meanwhile, Slade would escape to live out his life in some unsuspected haven.

To live. While the rest of them were consigned to their untimely graves, with their deaths put down to accident – not deliberate murder.

Carson frowned into the peaceful sky ahead, then consciously tried to relax. It would do no good to get tensed up and unable to concentrate. They were in a trap, but there must be some way out – there *had* to be.

Below them, in the distance, he saw the first faint gleam of the Channel through a rift in the clouds. Carson tried not to stare at it, lest Slade follow his gaze and realized how close they were to their goal. Cautiously, he set the controls for hover again, to gain a few more minutes before they were irrevocably out over the Channel.

Then he heard the thin, overriding sound, so faint at first that he could not quite identify it and feared that it was a change in the pitch of the engines portending further disaster. But the sound grew louder and, although he now realized what it was, he could not quite believe it. Someone was whistling back there, actually whistling.

> '*Oh, Genevieve, sweet Genevieve,*
> '*The days may come, the days may go . . .*'

Lillian identified the tune with a stab of jealousy. She glanced covertly at Paul and caught him half-smiling at Genevieve. But he had seen her and caught the hurt in her eyes. The whistling stopped abruptly.

Paul hadn't realized he'd been whistling until he saw Lillian's face change, then the burden of guilt weighed down on him again. His subconscious *would* have had to come up with that song. It wouldn't take a stroke of genius on Lillian's part to recognize that it must once have been 'our' song, back when 'our' did not embrace the same couple it did today.

Following on the guilt came a sharp flash of irritation. Why did Lillian have to be so upset and so *female* at a time like this? Surely she could not have imagined that he had married and lived with another woman and had a child with that woman without any love and affection? Or was it that the careless tune had brought it home to her too strongly? Of course there had been songs and signals, laughter and private jokes – especially in the early years. Back when there had been an air of excitement to every undertaking and one awoke in the morning anticipating the challenges the day would bring – with the sure certainty that one could meet every challenge and win.

Perhaps Genevieve was right. Perhaps life had been getting so dull and businesslike lately that he had unconsciously tried to put some spice back into it by rearranging his private life.

He couldn't complain of lack of challenge at the moment. He was face to face with the biggest challenge of his life. What was missing was any certainty that he might win through.

Genevieve smiled back at Paul; the haunting tune had penetrated the apathy into which she had sunk after her brief flare-up. He forgave her, then, for her stupidity in failing to get rid of Slade. It had been a clumsy, amateur attempt, she realized now. But what else could it have been?

Slade was the only one among them who was not an amateur at murder.

She closed her eyes against the sudden fear. Not fear for herself – although she, too, was too young to die – but fear for Sandy, so small and defenceless. The earlier fear that Sandy would die if they did not get her to a hospital was now replaced by the knowledge that they were all condemned to death.

How very ironic if she and Paul made it through to 'death do us part', after all.

TYCOON AND FAMILY WIPED OUT IN HELICOPTER CRASH. That was the way it would appear in newspaper headlines. Few people, apart from the solicitors concerned, knew that a divorce was in the offing. Lillian would only be mentioned as a faithful secretary, an employee flying with them on this occasion. Was it wicked to feel a faintly malicious satisfaction that the world would never know that the marriage had failed? They would die as man and wife – somehow the thought assuaged some of the pain. If only they could leave Sandy to build a life of her own.

Genevieve looked at Paul again, but he was staring thoughtfully at Slade, studying him. There remained the trace of a smile on his face. It was hard to believe, harder still to forgive, but in some grotesque way, Paul was enjoying the situation. At any moment, he might begin whistling again.

If they looked at each other once more and smiled in that way –

Lillian's fists clenched involuntarily. The cold steel

of nail file and corkscrew bit into the palm of her hand. She uncurled her fingers and withdrew the hand hastily from her pocket.

Had anyone noticed? She wondered if she looked guilty and made a conscious effort to smooth any expression from her face.

Not that anyone – that Slade – could know the reason for her action, but he must remain unsuspicious. When she made her move, she must take him completely by surprise.

Lillian remembered the crack as his gun struck Genevieve's head and shuddered. She had never encountered physical violence before, she was not sure that she was brave enough to face it. And yet, she had no choice. Violence had invaded her life, was standing here before her. With or without any action on her part, the violence would continue on its way to its inevitable end: the deaths of them all.

In any case, the others had been taken unawares when Genevieve launched herself so precipitately at Slade. If it happened again, surely Paul would join in the attack. The trouble was that Slade would be more prepared, too. This time, he would shoot.

If only they could look to the pilot for additional support. But he had his hands full with the helicopter. If the turbulence grew worse, he would have all he could do. But the turbulence seemed better now. In fact, the helicopter hardly seemed to be moving at all.

Lillian stiffened anxiously. What was wrong? Were they going to crash?

What did it matter? She forced herself to relax. Something terrible was going to happen to them anyway when Slade had his way. Perhaps a crash might be more merciful.

The helicopter lurched sideways and began chugging slowly forward again. False alarm.

Lillian found her muscles tensing: ready to scream, ready to spring. She bit down on incipient hysteria and took a deep breath, and then another. Wait ... patience ... the time was not ripe yet. But, when it was, would she be able to recognize the fact? Would she be ready? Could she act in time?

Carson tilted the Sikorsky from side to side as he allowed it to slide forward, giving the impression of moving against hostile air currents.

At the periphery of his field of vision, he detected the faint involuntary movements of concern from Slade and they helped harden his resolution as well as point the way to him.

They had to get rid of Slade – and in such a way that Slade did not kill them before they had a chance to get away from him.

Tightening his lips, Carson aimed the Sikorsky for the middle of the Channel, out of sight of either shoreline in this fog. With nothing but water beneath them and no sign of land, Slade would be disorientated, would have to depend on the reading of the instruments as relayed to him by the pilot. He had not enough technical knowledge to dispute what he was told, he would have to believe the man in command of the aircraft. *The pilot wants to live, too.*

But Slade did not intend that any of them should live.

The Channel slid beneath them, looking deceptively smooth from this height. The moonlight shimmered silver across its surface and fog had shredded out into decorative wisps that seemed to bear no menace. Another few miles out and they might disappear altogether – or might thicken into a solid fogbank again.

Abstractedly, Carson made a slight course correction, the best he could do without any assistance from ground control. It was too sudden and the aircraft bucked momentarily – perhaps his nerves were beginning to show.

'What are you doing?' Slade snarled.

'Trying to get us there in one piece,' Carson snarled back. 'I ought to radio ahead and – '

'No radio! If I have to say it again, I smash it!'

'On your head be it,' Carson shrugged. So long as the fog didn't thicken, they were probably safe enough. They were not high enough to interfere with any normal commercial flight lanes, nor low enough to risk colliding with any tall buildings once they were over land again.

But accidents could happen. Private aircraft could be flying at this altitude, thinking they were safe by having filed a flight plan and received clearance from either French or English officialdom. Carson wished there were some way he might risk one quick radio transmission without Slade's knowledge.

But that was impossible. Besides, it was safer not to.

Safe! Carson nearly laughed. There *was* no safety for them. They were all dead – or as good as. Once the helicopter had set Slade down on French territory, their life expectancy could be reckoned in seconds – the number of seconds it took to pull a trigger.

Their only safety lay up here in the air and they could not stay up indefinitely. Even if Slade did not grow restless at a protracted journey, they would eventually run out of fuel and have to come down. There was no way out for them.

Or was there one way?

CHAPTER XXVI

Carson squinted into the night sky ahead, trying to look as though he were concerned only with the immediate prospect. Trying to look as though he were not thinking at all, while his mind raced madly.

One way? One desperate chance? But all chances were desperate in this situation. Anything was worth a risk. Even the boss's wife had shown that she knew that when she had hurled herself at Slade.

The only chance they dare not take was the chance of trusting Slade, of believing the promises he held out that he would let them live.

Slade was going to kill them. But Slade might welcome the opportunity to save his bullets. Who knew how long a journey he still had before him? Obviously, he had made some plans, plans that called for a landing in France in the first place. Slade might feel safer on the journey still stretching before him if he could keep every piece of ammunition he now possessed. His need of it might be even greater in the future.

If Slade were to think that they were doomed already – without any further action on his part – the temptation to save ammunition might be a powerful one. Powerful enough to yield to.

If Slade could be convinced that the aircraft was in trouble . . . serious trouble. Trouble bad enough to force him to bail out and save himself . . . Then he might not bother to send any of his precious bullets into the rotor arm of an aircraft that was obviously going to crash in a matter of moments anyway.

It might just work.

It would be rough on the others, but they ought not to begrudge paying a few minutes of terror if it would buy them the rest of their lives.

In any case, there was no time to take a poll on the question. Whatever was to be done was best done while they were still over the Channel. The water was their friend.

Water . . . and altitude.

Casually, Carson tilted the pitch lever and set the aircraft climbing.

'What's happening?' Slade was growing increasingly jumpy. All to the good, if he were to be panicked into abandoning ship.

'Fog's thickening again,' Carson said. 'We want to get above it. It's a bastard down there tonight.'

Involuntarily Slade glanced downwards. As he did so, Carson leaned the fuel control to an overweak mixture. The piston engines gave a cough and the aircraft juddered.

'What's that?' Slade demanded.

'Probably nothing,' Carson said. *Time to start the alarm bells quivering.* 'But it may be a bastard up here, too. I told you we were running short of fuel. I've just had to switch to the emergency tank.'

'Then we'll have enough to get where we're going.'
Slade gave Carson a bleak smile. 'You can refuel after
I've left you.' The words were all right, but the tone was
false. 'You can even check in with your damned Air
Traffic Control people then and get wet-nursed all the
way back to Blighty.'

'Thanks,' Carson said tersely. 'I'll do just that.'
Slade laughed, sensing the disbelief but no longer
caring. It wouldn't be long now until the gloves were
off. 'That's right,' he said. 'You do just that.'

Carson looked back over his shoulder. It was
awfully quiet back there. They all seemed to be staring
into space – at nothing. Or were their lives passing
before those unseeing eyes? Was it the calm before a
storm of hysteria overtook one of the women again?
Or were they all genuinely becalmed by the recent
violence of their emotions?

Too bad he didn't know these people better. He'd
feel more confident if he could have had some idea of
their form in an emergency.

Then he nearly laughed again. An emergency! If
they weren't in the middle of one right now, what
would most people call it? And the passengers were
standing up to it very well. Especially the little French-
Canadian firebrand. What could the boss-man be
thinking of to want to trade her in on a newer model?
He didn't appreciate her – maybe he didn't deserve her.

'*Oh, Genevieve, sweet Genevieve* . . .' The abstracted
whistling started up again. Maybe Paul Jarvis was
beginning to appreciate his wife all over again. Or
remembering what he had seen in her in the first place.

'Shut up!' Slade snapped. The whistling stopped
abruptly on a dying fall that somehow conveyed

astonishment and reproach – and a realization that Slade's nerves weren't what they had been when this hi-jacking began.

Carson took advantage of Slade's divided attention to gain more altitude and to make a course correction that meant they were now following the Channel and no longer cutting across it. The manoeuvre would buy them just a little more time. Unless Slade noticed it.

Carson wondered whether the Sikorsky had yet shown up as an unidentified blip on someone's radar screen. He'd give a lot to be able to switch on the radio and find out if some Air Traffic Control Centre were frantically trying to raise him. And how long would it be before London Air Traffic Control realized that they were now overdue according to their flight plan? When they had been overdue a bit longer, London would automatically send out an alert asking other aircraft to be on the lookout for them.

There was not as much time as Carson had thought. There was a world out there – and they were only momentarily lost to it. When the world came looking for them – as it must to keep its air lanes clear – the danger would be increased.

Carson tilted the control again and grabbed for a few hundred more feet of sky.

Paul Jarvis frowned as he felt the aircraft surge beneath him. The pilot – Carson, yes, Carson – seemed to be handling the helicopter in an increasingly erratic manner. Could the man be cracking up under the strain? Or was he having more of a problem with the rotors than he was willing to admit to his passengers? The way those engines had behaved a few minutes ago had not seemed healthy.

Well, no point in worrying about that. It was out of his hands – Carson was the man in control of the aircraft. *Correction: Carson merely had the aircraft in his hands – Slade was the man in control.*

And Paul Jarvis was nowhere. The big tycoon, the star of the FT Index, the ex-whizz-kid before whom corporations trembled and stockbrokers toadied, was sitting here on his overstuffed seat as helpless as . . . As helpless as little Sandy, stretched out across the seats in front and, mercifully, unconscious at the moment.

Paul could feel eyes on him, but refused to look up and meet them. What reassurance had he to give to Genevieve or Lillian? Or even Sandy? *'Never mind, dear, I'll just write out a cheque'? 'Don't worry, darling, Daddy will kiss it and make it better'?*

He was powerless. It was not a pleasant feeling. Nor was it one he was accustomed to.

The engines spluttered again and the Sikorsky gave a lurch sideways. Slade glared at everyone impartially as though, in some way, it would be everyone's fault but his if anything went wrong with his plans. It always was, with types like that.

As Paul remembered the case, it had been a particularly nasty one. Slade, on the borderline of sanity, had seemed to take delight in slaughter. Furthermore, there had been a great deal of money involved – money never recovered and, presumably, hidden away somewhere waiting for him to reclaim it.

No, there would be no use offering Slade money again. Slade required their deaths more than their money. There could be no bargaining with him.

144 TIGHTROPE FOR THREE

Neither, he admitted to himself, did he want to bargain with Slade. All he wanted to do with Slade was kill him.

He caught himself pursing his mouth to whistle again and hurriedly straightened his lips. Not only was whistling an irritation to Slade, but the tune still haunting his mind was *Sweet Genevieve* – which would wound Lillian. Some time – if they had any time – after this nightmare was over, he must try to explain to Lillian and make it up to her. It was not that he loved her less, it was simply that no one seemed to have written any songs about girls named Lillian. Perhaps he could try '*Lily of Laguna*'.

But whistling wasn't allowed. Slade preferred his captives silent.

Perhaps it was best that way. No letting off steam. Instead, let the head of anger build up in him. Slade was a poor psychologist – it would have been better to let his captives distract themselves in any way they could, rather than force them to dwell on their predicament.

Slade wasn't a psychologist. Slade was a killer.

Abruptly the engines spluttered again and the clatter of the rotors changed in some way.

Carson suddenly became frantically busy, his arms moving wildly, his head swinging the width of the instrument panel and back, although his spine remained rigid. He was making soft, senseless sounds, not quite words, as though trying to curse the aircraft and encourage it at the same time.

'What's the matter?' Slade kicked at the pilot's seat, demanding attention. 'What's happening?'

'The bastard is cutting out!' Carson's head turned so

that they could see his taut pale face. 'The rear torque motor is trying to cut out!'

'What does that mean?' Slade demanded.

In answer, the aircraft pivoted slowly on its own axis.

'What's that?' Slade screamed as Carson turned back to his instruments and surreptitiously removed his foot from the rudder. 'What's going on?'

'The rear rotor keeps the aircraft straight and steady. It corrects the torque.' Carson spoke between clenched teeth, keeping the engineering principle as simple as possible so that even Slade could follow it. 'When you have a powerful overhead rotor turning in one direction, the body of the aircraft wants to go in the other direction to counterbalance it. That's why helicopters took so much longer than the fixed-wing aircraft to develop. It wasn't until it was discovered that a rear torque rotor would correct the balance that the helicopter became a practical proposition – '

'I didn't ask for a goddamned history lesson!' Slade raged. 'I want to know what's going to happen *now*. To this helicopter. To us.'

'That's an even more basic engineering principle,' Carson said. ' "What goes up must come down." '

'And us? What about us?'

'Oh, we'll come down too,' Carson said.

'*Do* something – ' Slade drummed frantically on the back of Carson's seat. '*Do* something!'

'I am doing something,' Carson said. 'I'm trying to keep us up.'

The cabin revolved again with slowly increasing speed.

'Land!' Slade ordered. 'Get us away from the water

and land the damned thing.'

'I can't set her down like this.' Carson nudged the rudder pedal again and gave the aircraft another spin for emphasis. If the rear torque rotor really *had* cut out, they wouldn't still be in the air arguing. Failure of that rotor was the reason for most helicopter crashes. But Slade wouldn't know that. And the mild aerobatics were quite enough to unnerve the unwary. Carson pressed home the point.

'We'd crash – with *no* survivors. Staying over the water is our best hope. We're going to have to ditch. We've got a better chance going down on water than on land.'

'Going down?' The drumming on the seat stopped abruptly. Carson knew that Slade was staring past his shoulder, down at the murky deep waters of the Channel below. 'Down *there?*'

There was a soft whimper, as though in endorsement, from the unconscious child.

Carson risked a glance back over his shoulder. The women were both pale, but standing up to the strain. Obviously neither was going to give way to panic in front of the other. So that was all right. Genevieve was hunching protectively over her child. Carson wished there were some way he could reassure her.

Paul Jarvis was sitting upright, taut with the peculiar tension of a man poised for flight or fight – and frustrated by the knowledge that there was nowhere to run and no one to fight. He was powerless in this situation: everything was in the hands of the pilot – or the lap of the gods.

'You'd better break out the life-raft,' Carson said, carefully not designating anyone for the task.

'There's a life-raft?' Slade's voice quivered with relief.

'A big one,' Carson confirmed. 'Big enough for ten people. It will take all of us. And it's self-inflating as it hits the water. All we have to do is shove it out the door and jump into it. I ought to be able to hold us steady above it long enough for that. Then I'll take the helicopter further away, so it won't sink the raft as it comes down, set it on automatic and try to get clear myself before the crash.'

It was a good plan. It might even have worked. If Slade would have allowed the others into the life-raft. But Slade was no hero and it was unlikely that he subscribed to any such nonsense as 'women and children first'. Slade would be the first one into that lovely large life-raft, which would beckon to him from the waters of the Channel like a welcoming island.

Once on board, he would not let the others off the aircraft. Why should he, when a crash would finish his work for him? If the helicopter sank into the Channel with everyone on board, Slade needn't waste any ammunition. He could sit safely in the life-raft and paddle the rest of the distance to France. It was a tailor-made solution for him.

The trouble was, would he suspect it?

'I'll get the life-raft out,' Paul volunteered with enthusiasm, the prospect of something to do giving him fresh hope. Perhaps, in the confusion of the transfer from helicopter to life-raft, Slade could be overpowered. He started from his seat.

'Get back there!' Slade snapped. '*You're* not going to get anything!' He waved the gun. 'Except a bullet, if you don't keep quiet and let me think.'

'Think fast,' Carson said. 'We don't have all that much time.'

The slowly increasing carousel motion of the aircraft seemed to confirm his statement.

'Where *is* the life-raft?' Slade demanded.

'It's stowed in a locker at the rear.' Paul answered slowly, reluctantly. But the life-raft was their only chance. Or was it? Already he was beginning to suspect what Carson already knew: that Slade had no intention of allowing anyone else into the life-raft with him. Paul hoped the women didn't realize it. Perhaps it was unkind to let them go on hoping, but he felt that anything that could postpone the full anguish of realizing their true position –

Paul looked up and met Lillian's eyes. She looked away quickly, almost guiltily, as though to spare him the pain of knowing that she knew. Ruefully, he felt the familiar admiration for her: you couldn't keep anything from Lillian. Not for long. She had one of the best brains in the business. Her acumen had done much to secure the English market for him. But, for her own sake, he wished at this moment that she could have been just a bit slower on the uptake. Just this once. He would have preferred to spare her this.

'It's a concealed locker,' Paul said. His mouth twisted wryly. 'The designer didn't want to spoil the look of the cabin by anything too blatant. I can – '

'You'll do nothing,' Slade said. He looked around desperately, bracing himself as the fuselage rotated again.

'I – ' Lillian's voice broke. She ran her tongue over her dry lips and tried again. 'I know where it is. It's in the hatch just under the bar. I can get it out for you.'

'That's more like it,' Slade said. 'A little of the *right* kind of co-operation around here. That's what we need.' He gestured her out of her seat with the gun. 'Go and get it, blondie.'

Lillian got to her feet unsteadily and walked towards the rear of the cabin, clutching at the backs of seats along the way to help keep her balance.

Slade watched her go, then turned to survey the others, no longer bothering to hide the calculation in his eyes.

'Okay,' Carson said. 'Now, when she gets the life-raft out, position it in front of the door. I want it to go out as the door opens. We're going to have to work fast to abandon this craft before she sinks — '

He hoped he sounded as though he still believed Slade was likely to share the life-raft. Once Slade was out of the helicopter, he *was* going to have to work fast. It would be a variation of a bird's broken-wing routine. He'd have to lift the helicopter again — as though it were struggling out of his control — and try to skitter along just above the surface of the water, making it look as though the helicopter might plunge into the Channel at any second, so that Slade wouldn't be tempted to shoot. Only, instead of luring the hunters away from the brood in the nest, he'd be taking the whole brood to safety with him — he hoped.

Once they were out of range of Slade's gun, they could resume altitude, radio Air Traffic Control, tell them what had happened and get them to notify the police. They could then continue with their interrupted flight and get the kid to hospital, leaving the police to come and collect Slade from his precious life-raft. Like a sitting duck.

Lillian seemed to be taking a long time with the life-raft. Carson glanced back, but she was out of sight at the extreme rear of the cabin with the intervening seats blocking his line of vision. He gave the helicopter another slow spin just to keep Slade worried.

'There.' Lillian stumbled forward with the cumbersome bundle that was the life-raft and deposited it at the door. Paul had watched her struggling to get the awkward heavy rubber life-raft out of the locker and cursed himself for not being able to help her. She looked drained and exhausted by the effort. He met her eyes and smiled encouragingly, but she flushed and looked away. Did she feel a traitor for having done anything to assist Slade? But there had been no option, really. One way or another, Slade would have secured the life-raft and made sure of being its only occupant.

Anyway, it would be an improvement to have Slade out of the aircraft. A man ought to have a choice of the company he died in. Slade would not be anyone's choice.

Carson looked back over his shoulder again and decided that it was time to precipitate the action.

'Get down by the door and stand by to open it,' Carson directed. 'I'll take her down and hold her as steady as I can while all of you clear out. Remember, throw the life-raft out first. It will inflate as it hits the surface. Jump into it, if you can. If not, jump as close to it as possible and those already in will pull you aboard.'

'Stay where you are — ' Slade warned the others, moving towards the door.

Agonized, Paul watched the slow realization dawning in Genevieve's eyes.

'No — ' Genevieve fought against the realization,

unbuckling the seat-belts holding Sandy in place, trying to gather up the unconscious child.

'Help me – ' she appealed to Paul. 'Carry her down. When M'sieu Slade gets into the life-raft, you can lower Sandy down to him, so that she is not jarred, so that she does not get wet – '

'Stay where you are!' Slade ordered again, as Paul instinctively tried to move.

'You cannot – ' Genevieve turned her pleading, accusing eyes on Slade. 'The child has done no harm. She doesn't understand what has happened. She doesn't even know. She's been unconscious most of the time. You *must* take her with you.'

All eyes upon him, Slade wavered, then recovered himself. 'Are you crazy?' he snarled. 'A sick kid, bouncing around in a little life-raft on that cold water? What kind of a chance would she have?'

Genevieve refused to be fooled, she looked at him steadily. 'A better chance than in this helicopter, *n'est-ce pas?*'

Slade looked away quickly and opened his mouth as though to deny it, but no words came out.

Paul watched them closely, not daring to move or draw attention to himself in any way, afraid to disturb the tenuous understanding growing between them. If Sandy were to be saved, then he would not feel quite so bitter at his own existence coming to so abrupt and senseless an end. If something could be salvaged from the wreck, if Sandy were to go on . . .

Carson looked over his shoulder and choked back a curse. Slade was wavering. The woman was going to ruin everything – and there was no way he could warn her, no way to let her know that once Slade was out of the aircraft, everything would be all right.

But if he took the kid with him –

'*Please* . . .' There were tears in Genevieve's eyes. 'She's all we have. She can do you no harm – '

Carson sideslipped the aircraft and dropped it several feet. Lillian screamed involuntarily.

'Get ready to ditch,' Carson said urgently. 'I can't hold this thing in the air much longer.'

Even if Slade *did* take Sandy with him, Paul realized, there was no guarantee that he would not tip her over the side of the life-raft as soon as the helicopter had gone down. The empty life-raft could be pushed back into the water upside-down after Slade had landed in France and a body showing up some distance away would occasion no surprise. Perhaps other bodies would float free of the helicopter and be found elsewhere. *Their* bodies. With a detached sense of unreality, Paul looked at the two women he had loved.

'No!' Slade was at the door now, the life-raft at his feet like a bundle of rags. Like a dead body.

'*Please* – ' Genevieve sobbed.

'Hurry it up!' Carson snapped off the engines. The sudden deadly silence was more terrifying than anything that had gone before. The passengers weren't to know that autorotation was a standard and perfectly safe manoeuvre, the helicopter windmilling down with the pilot still in complete control.

'We're losing altitude,' Carson said unnecessarily, as the helicopter began to descend.

Paul closed his eyes and prayed – concentrated – whatever you wanted to call it when you were face to face with the Unknown, with the biggest gamble life ever offered you.

'*Mummy* . . .' Sandy struggled upright in Genevieve's arms. She opened her eyes and gazed around blankly, obviously not registering anything she saw. Beyond seeing, beyond hearing—nearly beyond help. '*Mummy*—' Her eyes closed again and she sank back in Genevieve's arms.

'*Please.*' Genevieve's voice was barely a whisper. '*Oh, please.*'

Slade looked from one to the other, shaking his head in negation, then abruptly capitulated. 'Oh, all right,' he said. 'All right.'

'*Aaah.*' Genevieve sank back against her seat, clutching Sandy tightly – for the last time. 'Thank you, M'sieu Slade. Thank you.'

She was thanking him! Paul tensed with fury. *Thanking* the man who was going to take her life – take all their lives – merely because she had his spurious assurance that he would – for the moment – save her child.

'Right!' Slade fumbled at the catch of the door, fighting against the airstream to open it. 'Get her up here. Be ready to toss her down as soon as the life-raft starts inflating. But none of you – ' he waved the gun to emphasize his point – 'had better think of trying to come with her.'

'No . . .' Lillian wailed in anguish. '*Oh no!*'

'I'm not so bad,' Slade said defensively. 'Why do you want to act as if I'm some kind of monster?' He glared at Lillian. 'I'll see the kid's okay.'

'*No-o-o,*' Lillian wailed again.

'Thank you.' Half-dragging, half-carrying Sandy, Genevieve evaded Lillian's restraining grasp and stood beside Slade with quiet triumph.

'*Oh no!*' Lillian seemed unable to say anything else, to make any more coherent comment.

Paul was suddenly alert, sensing danger. Why didn't Lillian want Sandy to go with Slade?

'What's the matter?' Slade, too, was abruptly wary. 'Don't you *want* the kid to be saved?'

'Not down there. The water will be so cold. You can't – ' Lillian broke off, shaking her head wordlessly.

'We're wasting time,' Slade said. The aircraft tilted perilously and he swore. 'Help me with this door,' he ordered Genevieve.

'No!' Lillian stumbled forward, catching at Genevieve's shoulder. 'Don't! Don't let him take her! Let him go alone!'

'Why?' Slade was sharply suspicious. 'Don't you believe I'm human? Or – ' his eyes narrowed coldly – 'or do you have a better reason? What do you know that we don't know?'

'You can't let her go with him,' Lillian implored Genevieve.

'It's her only chance,' Genevieve said stubbornly.

'It's no chance at all,' Lillian said. 'Oh God!' She brought her clenched fist out of her pocket.

'Don't you see?' She opened her hand. The nail file and corkscrew fell to the floor with a light clatter, and lay there gleaming dully.

'That life-raft will never stay afloat. I – I bored holes in it with . . . with *those*. I – I meant to kill *him*!'

Carson sighed softly and switched the engines back into action.

CHAPTER XXVII

'Come here, Lillian,' Slade said softly.

Genevieve began dragging Sandy back to the comparative safety of the seats.

Lillian paled, but lifted her chin defiantly and moved slowly towards Slade.

Slade reached out and caught the front of her blouse, pulling her forward sharply. 'You tried to kill me,' he snarled. He began to shake her, watching her head snap back and forth, wanting to shake away the contempt in her eyes. He forgot the gun in his other hand – besides, a gun wasn't personal enough. Not for the score he had to settle with this one.

'You – ' His voice rose incredulously. '*You* tried to kill *me*.'

'Why not, M'sieu Slade?' Genevieve asked coldly, from the shelter of the seat she had regained. '*You* intend to kill *us*.'

The flimsy blouse ripped and he was left with a strip of material in his hand. He flung Lillian away from him. She twisted and fell face down, striking her chin on the arm of one of the seats.

Slade pushed past her, waving the gun warningly at anyone who might try to stop him, and slumped down in the co-pilot's seat again. He levelled the gun at them over the back of the seat.

Lillian had struggled to a sitting position. He saw with satisfaction the thin trickle of blood from the corner of her mouth. She had probably only bitten her lip when she struck against the arm of the chair. It was enough for now, it had to be. But later –

'Oh, Lillian,' he promised softly, 'Lillian, you've got something really special waiting for you when we land.'

Paul handed Lillian his handkerchief, Genevieve held a mirror for her while she hastily tried to repair the damage. It was as though they realized that the sight of blood was inflaming Slade, in the way that blood drew sharks to a wounded swimmer. Slade's madness seemed increasingly near the surface now. And the realization that his victims were not going to their fates tamely, but intended to fight back all the way, seemed to be maddening him even more.

Yet what did he expect? Paul wondered briefly about Slade's earlier victims. Had Slade never encountered resistance before?

This was why it was said that violence breeds violence. Paul looked again at the two women in his life: both gentle, pretty, doll-like even; from comfortable backgrounds, secure homes. Certainly neither had ever encountered violence before – and yet they were fighting back as though they had been born and raised in the jungle. He was proud of them both.

But what was *he* doing? Genevieve had tried with both claws and drugged coffee; Lillian had tried by puncturing the life-raft; and the pilot, Carson – good man, Carson, damned good man – was in there trying every minute. There was a great future for Carson in EngAm International – if any of them had a future.

It was just bad luck that none of the tricks had worked. Bad luck – and lack of communication. If any of them had been able to know what the other was planning, they might have brought it off. They might even now be safe in England, instead of waiting to crash in this spinning aircraft –

Wait a minute! What had happened to the aircraft? It was no longer spinning.

'Hey!' Slade spotted it at almost the same moment. 'What's going on here?' He glared at Carson suspiciously. 'Why aren't we still turning around?'

'We got lucky,' Carson said tersely, not looking at him, defying Slade to call him a liar. 'The rear rotor just snapped back into operation again.'

'So we're not going to crash, after all?' Slade brought the gun round to a point just behind Carson's ear.

'Not yet,' Carson said.

'Lucky, eh?' Slade snapped back the safety-catch on the gun, the sharp click almost as decisive as a bullet. 'I ought to – '

'I wouldn't advise it,' Carson said. 'Not unless you can fly this thing. It would be a pity for you to get this far and then blow it all because you couldn't keep your temper, wouldn't it?' Without waiting for an answer, he tilted and dropped the helicopter for emphasis.

'All right.' Slade let the safety-catch fall into place reluctantly. 'I'll settle the score with you too when we land.'

'Which may be sooner than you think,' Carson said.

'What?' Slade peered down through the Plexiglass window. There was still nothing but water and mist below. 'Where are we?'

'I'm not sure,' Carson tried again. 'You won't let me get a radio fix – '

'No radio!' Slade snapped automatically.

'Have it your way,' Carson shrugged. 'But we're running out of fuel.'

'How can we be? France isn't that far. If you — '

'I'd already used up a lot of the fuel flying down from London,' Carson reminded him. 'And I had to switch over to the emergency tank some time ago. That's getting low now.'

Genevieve leaned forward and touched Lillian on the arm. 'Thank you,' she murmured.

'For what?' Lillian was startled.

'For confessing as you did.' Genevieve looked at her earnestly. 'For not letting him take Sandy into that life-raft. It was very brave of you — '

'No, it wasn't,' Lillian said. 'There was nothing else I could have done.'

'You could have let her go.'

'No,' Lillian said. 'I couldn't have done that.'

Genevieve smiled and leaned back, conscious of a sense of healing. She found that, for the first time, she could visualize a future in which she would see Sandy go off to visit her father and his new wife without any feeling of pain and foreboding. Sandy would be safe with this woman, she could trust her to look after her properly.

Furthermore, she could in time welcome Lillian's children into her own home when they visited Canada. They would, after all, be Sandy's half-brothers and sisters. It was right that Sandy's home should also be theirs when they chose to visit. They were all part of one family — or would be.

She looked across at Paul and smiled. A new smile.

Goodbye and hello. She had made the final transition.
Did he understand?

They had guts, his women. Paul returned Genevieve's
tremulous smile and saw her turn to say something
quietly to Lillian. There was a sense of new alliance in
the atmosphere. If they got out of this in one piece, a
lot of things were going to be different. Better.

If. The old doomed feeling of guilt swept over him
again. What was *he* doing about it? The others had all
made an effort. If only it had been a concerted effort, it
might have succeeded.

But he – what had *he* done? He had been sitting
here, doing nothing. Only a trifle less helpless than
Sandy lying unconscious across the seats. And about as
useless. What price a Captain of Industry in this
situation?

They would have no chance of taking Slade by
surprise again. He was thoroughly on his guard now,
danger signals flaring in his narrow eyes. He would
shoot first. Nor would there be another chance to bluff
him into abandoning the aircraft. He wouldn't fall for
that trick twice.

He had taken them by surprise in the beginning.
That action had given Slade the whip-hand and he had
held it ever since. With no time to plan, no way to
communicate, they might as well be locked into
separate cells with Slade as their jailer.

And yet, some communication had been achieved.
They all knew now that they were united in one desire:
the desire to see Slade dead. To kill Slade, either acting
individually or in unison.

The trouble was, Slade knew it too.

Slade was keeping them under a steady malevolent surveillance, his head turning slowly from one to the other, his eyes cold. He seemed almost to be waiting for an excuse to begin shooting. It was hard to tell which of them had roused him to this pitch of fury, but when the shooting started, the opening choice would be between Lillian and Carson. And Carson was needed to fly the aircraft.

Carson adjusted the pitch as the helicopter tilted unexpectedly. His movement was a little too abrupt and Slade turned to him sharply, suspicious.

'What's happening?' he demanded.

'Nothing new,' Carson said. 'We're still running out of fuel.'

After he'd said it, Carson experienced a cold unnerving moment when he wondered if he'd have time to regret it. Slade's eyes flashed murder, his finger tightened on the trigger – only at the last second had the self-protective instinct snapped into action, reminding Slade that, if the aircraft went down, he went down with it. With a visible effort, the finger eased on the trigger, but the eyes remained colder than ever.

'Watch it,' Slade said, with the dangerous softness that was more deadly than a shout. 'Just watch it.'

'I am.' Carson's eyes locked on the fuel gauge. 'We've got, possibly, another half-hour. If we're lucky.'

'If we aren't – ?'

Carson glanced downward through the Plexiglass nose. The Channel still gleamed below them, although off in the distance a darker, duller mass hinted at a shoreline.

'We were "lucky" once before,' Slade whispered.

'We'd better be again.'

'Maybe we will be,' Carson admitted.

'That's better.' Slade leaned back in the co-pilot's seat, almost relaxing. But the gun still pointed un-waveringly at Carson.

Carson tried to keep his face expressionless, hoping it would pass for calm. Out of the corner of his eye, he saw Slade scan the control panel anxiously, but it was quite obvious that Slade might as well be looking at ancient tablets inscribed in Sanskrit. He had no idea at all of what he was seeing – the dials and graphs con-veyed nothing to him.

Which was just as well.

There was only one small point in their favour now. Slade, dizzy and disorientated, had lost whatever sense of direction he might originally have possessed. He did not realize the truth.

They were no longer headed for France. The fog-shrouded mainland they were approaching was the coast of England.

It might do them no practical good at all, but Carson felt minimally safer for the fact and wished that he could convey it to the others. When they landed, it would be on English soil.

Whatever happened to them, Slade would not find it so easy to escape again.

But it was nearly dawn. Even though Slade might be too disorientated to notice whether the sun were rising in the east or the west – and too city-bred to recognize the difference – even he would notice if he saw a Union Jack fluttering from a flagpole instead of a Tricolor. Carson hoped that the fog would still be thick enough to disguise any identifiable discrepancies in terrain or townships until it was too late.

Too late for what?

Too late for Slade to act. But, if Slade believed himself to be safely in France, he would have no hesitation in killing them. If he realized that he had been betrayed and brought back to England, he would kill them just as quickly – and perhaps less mercifully.

Heads I win, tails you lose.

But a posthumous revenge was better than none at all. Slade would not find it so easy to get away from England again. By this time, his escape must have been discovered and the manhunt would be on.

'What's that?' Slade leaned forward, staring out into the night, trying to pinpoint the source of the new noise that was steadily coming closer.

'What?' Carson had been too immersed in his own thoughts to notice, but now that Slade had alerted him he recognized the sound – although he was not willing to admit it quite yet – and identified its source.

They were no longer alone in the sky.

'Over there!' Slade pointed with the gun. 'A plane! Coming towards us. Who is it?'

'Perhaps the Air Force, perhaps Customs and Excise, or Immigration. Perhaps the police. How do I know?' Carson bluffed. 'A lot of people get nervous at an unidentified aircraft roaming around in their air space.'

'What do they want?' Slade glared outwards, as though he would intimidate them, too.

'They want to know who we are, what we're doing here, where we think we're going. The usual things.' Carson shrugged, trying to appear casual. 'They're probably trying to raise us on the radio right now.'

It wasn't quite true. The chances were that it was just another casual aircraft. Even if the Sikorsky were showing up as a blip on someone's radar screen, they wouldn't be sending out interceptor planes. There were too many Sunday drivers of the air around for that. Air Traffic Control Centre would try to raise them by radio and, if they didn't succeed, would route other aircraft around the stranger, meanwhile logging the time and watching the direction it was taking. After which they would circulate airports in the vicinity and there would presently be a very regretful Sunday driver.

But Slade wouldn't know normal procedures.

'Don't touch that!' Slade had been waiting for Carson to make a move towards the radio again. He knocked Carson's hand aside with the gun. 'Make them go away.'

'You'll have to make up your mind,' Carson sighed. 'Do you want radio silence, or do you want them to go away? One or the other, you can't have both.' Unnoticed by Slade, he flashed his landing lights as a distress signal to the other aircraft.

The plane approached them carefully, keeping well beyond collision range – and firing distance. Just as well. Slade looked ready to fire off a couple of potshots. Then the fat would really be in the fire.

'How did they find us?' Slade glared at Carson suspiciously. 'How did you let them know?'

'Be your age,' Carson said. 'They have radar – that's why we have to file flight plans, so they can keep track of who's where and identify planes as they show up on the screen. They can't have people cruising wherever they feel like it and crossing international routes and colliding with scheduled airliners.'

Slade still looked unconvinced. Carson turned to watch the oncoming plane, trying to keep one eye on Slade. There was no telling what that maniac would do next now that the pressure was mounting.

There was a light flashing erratically from the other aircraft now. They had obviously given up hope of trying to make radio contact and were trying visual signals on the chance that the Sikorsky's radio was out of commission. *Nothing so simple, friends.*

'We ought to answer them,' Carson said. 'They won't be happy until we do.'

The airplane began circling them cautiously, still blinking out an invitation to confide in them.

Carson knew that they would be noting down the identification stencilled on the side of the helicopter and radioing back to base for information about it. Soon, very soon, they would have all the information, from the name of the company registering the Sikorsky to the original flight plan.

'What are they doing now?' Slade asked.

'Just looking us over,' Carson said evenly. He wondered whether the observers in the plane could see Slade's gun and begin to get an inkling of the situation. They must be watching the helicopter very sharply — couldn't they put two and two together?

'Get rid of them!' Slade ordered.

'Yes, sir. Right away, sir.' Carson was too exasperated to worry about tact. 'I'll just snap my fingers and they'll disappear.'

'Don't get — '

Carson flicked at the light switch and the helicopter was abruptly plunged into darkness. Someone gasped behind them, then the cabin lights went on again.

Blinking in the sudden brilliance, Carson hoped that the other aircraft had been able to observe Slade's gun raised and pointed at his head just as the lights came on again. *That* ought to give them the message they'd been looking for.

The plane circled them once again slowly, then dipped a wing and veered off.

'Where are they going?' Slade demanded.

'Back to base, I suppose.'

'Why?'

'Perhaps they're running out of fuel too.' Carson hoped he sounded convincing. The other plane would be trying to check out the information they had gathered. *Had* they seen that the pilot was being threatened? With any luck, they'd notify the right authorities and start things happening.

But what could even the right authorities do? A siege on land and the police would surround the place and outwait the gunman. Time was on their side. In the air, with a limited fuel capacity, time was on no one's side.

'They'll be back,' Carson warned. 'We still haven't told them what they want to know.'

'We're not going to.' Slade looked around, as though seeking help. 'And we're not going to be here when they get back. Change course.'

'That won't do any good.' Automatically Carson changed course. They were over land now, so it didn't matter. 'They'll still be able to track us.'

'Not if you drop down below the radar coverage.

'You mean land here?' Carson asked hopefully.

'Not land, no. Keep going. Get away from the radar

fix they've got on us – and keep it low so that they can't get another fix.'

'You're crazy,' Carson said flatly. He looked down at the woolly white mist hiding the ground from sight. 'We can't go hedge-hopping in this fog.'

'Down!' Slade's voice was deadly. He meant it.

Carson glanced quickly at his set face and then began to lose altitude.

CHAPTER XXVIII

Paul watched the thick white mist swoop closer, as though it would rise and envelop them completely. Perhaps that might be the best thing. Crash. No more problems. Let everybody else worry about the state of the world, the Company, the next thing to do.

Carson was a damned good pilot, but was he good enough to keep the helicopter in the air when a maniac who understood nothing about aeronautics was giving impossible orders? Even Carson seemed to doubt it. He was looking more concerned than he had at any time since the hi-jacking started. How much longer *would* their fuel hold out?

In an unguarded moment Paul allowed himself to catch Genevieve's eyes. She was frowning and did not respond to the encouraging smile he gave her. She was taking Sandy's pulse and she looked across at him and shook her head slightly. There was additional cause for concern there, as well. The only thing to be thankful for was that Sandy was still unconscious and would not know anything about it when they went down.

He became aware that Lillian was trying to attract his attention. Reluctantly, he met her eyes.

I'm sorry, she mouthed.

He shook his head. *He* should be apologizing to *her.* To all of them. He had done nothing – could do nothing. Slade had been keeping watch on him continuously, reckoning him as the likeliest source of danger, discounting the two women almost entirely. Slade had learned his mistake now and was watching them all impartially. But still Paul could do nothing, be of no use. It was a chastening experience.

His turn would have to come when the helicopter set down. Before Slade had a chance to cripple it. If he could attract Slade's fire, make him use all the bullets, then perhaps the others would have a chance.

Paul looked away, lest Lillian read the intention in his eyes and try to stop him. Genevieve would be more practical. If she thought it would ensure Sandy's survival, she would allow him to sacrifice himself.

Provided he got the chance. They were dropping rapidly now, trying to sink beneath the radar sweep. The ground below was completely hidden by the thick sea fog. It might be more luck than judgement if they didn't smash into a tree or hilltop.

Was Carson flying on instruments? The Sikorsky was equipped with the best instruments money could buy, Paul knew; he had paid for them. But he found he had no idea of their capacity. He hadn't paid attention – money, but not attention. He had known intellectually that his life might depend on them some day, but he had never really believed it. He hoped now that his money had been well spent.

The helicopter stopped descending abruptly just

above the thick mist and began scuttling along over the top of the fog. In another minute they would be well away from any radar fix the authorities had had on them. Away from the possibility of outside help again. The brief flare of optimism began to die. They were on their own again. They always had been.

There seemed darker patches here and there in the fog below. Treetops? High buildings? Impossible to tell – until it was too late. If they went too low and in the wrong spot, their landing gear might be ripped away. How could they land in this?

The helicopter wavered and began to move upwards again, as though the same thought had occurred to Carson.

'Don't try anything funny!' Slade said sharply.

'Don't worry, we're still beneath the radar.' Carson kept climbing. 'They won't find us again.' He wished it weren't true. Glancing down, he was momentarily frozen as the fog thickened, rose, and even enveloped the instrument panel in front of him.

Carson blinked, took a deep breath, closed his eyes for a moment, then opened them. The mist swirled and thinned, the instrument panel swam into focus again. Fatigue. His eyes were blurring with fatigue – and, possibly, the strain under which he was attempting to function.

If his eyes were betraying him, what was happening with his brain?

He had had no sleep since – Dizziness assailed Carson as he tried to work out the timing. Twenty-four hours? Thirty hours? Longer? He had not officially been on duty and that marathon card game had seemed like a good idea, especially as he had been winning. So far as anyone in the Company had known, Paul Jarvis was safely in Canada, as was his wont at this time of year. There had been no reason, then, to worry about getting enough sleep. Although he was theoretically on call, in practice the Board of Directors, who were also entitled to his services, were comfortably ensconced in their London clubs, enjoying the run-up to the Festive Season, and unlikely to require the use of the Executive Helicopter until after New Year's Day, when they might decide on a flip over to the Riviera or to the currently fashionable ski resort.

Who could blame a helicopter pilot, then – a mere employee – if he followed the example of his lords and masters and relaxed completely when it appeared that no one would care about it – or even know about it?

Then there had come that sudden telephone call from Harlow. Carson suppressed a groan. It had been some prize packet he had drawn. He blinked again and was only mildly reassured to find that his eyesight was still clear. The inner fog could close in on him again at any moment, he knew. And the fog below was bad enough.

Was it thinning in the distance? Or was it just the first faint streaks of dawn giving that illusion?

Abruptly, Sandy began screaming.

Carson twisted round. The child was trying to sit up, clutching at her stomach. The screams were chilling and urgent.

'Shut that kid up!' Slade snapped.

'*Mon Dieu!* It's rupturing!' Genevieve wailed.

The helicopter engines choked and spluttered.

'Hold on tight, folks,' Carson said. 'This is the end of the line.'

There was no time for argument, no time for prayer —
although Carson could hear Genevieve murmuring
something in French, or perhaps Latin. He couldn't
spare the concentration needed to differentiate. Whatever it was, it couldn't do any harm.

The child kept screaming all through the descent.
And Carson was with her all the way. He felt like
screaming himself *The pilot wants to live, too.* If she
knew what he knew, she'd be screaming even louder.

The fog enveloped them, thick and blinding.
Visibility couldn't have been worse if they had come
down in the middle of the Channel and were sinking
into its waters.

Carson had always preferred a visual to an instrument landing, but now there was no choice. Feeling as
helpless as Paul Jarvis, Carson gentled the instrument
controls, sinking slowly through the fog.

Lady Luck was with them. Perhaps she had decided
it was time to put in a late, guilt-ridden appearance to
try to make up for what she had done in saddling them
with Slade.

The landing gear connected with solid earth. At
least, he presumed it was solid earth, although in this
fog, it could equally well be a flat rooftop or the edge of
a cliff. On a night like this, Carson was prepared to
make no comfortable assumptions, accept no guarantees.

The Sikorsky bounced skittishly into the air and
came down again — still on solid ground. Perhaps they
had made it, after all.

He didn't turn off the engines, the rotors continued
to whirl slowly, regardless of the fuel being eaten
away.

The adults in the aircraft looked at each other with a

curiously shared triumph. They had made it. Even the child's screams abated to a whimper – but an agonizing whimper with an urgency that had not been apparent before. Sandy's situation had changed, worsened – she must take top priority now.

'Right!' Slade rose to his feet, taking command, reminding them who was in charge, who really took priority. His gun reinforced his claim. 'Everybody stay where you are.'

The small relieved movements anticipating freedom abruptly stopped. For a brief moment they had been ordinary passengers, sharing a dangerous landing. Now Slade had reminded them.

The landing had been accomplished, but the danger had not yet passed.

'On your feet, Lillian.' Slade gestured with the gun. 'No,' he levelled it at the others. 'Nobody else. Just Lillian.' He leered at her. 'We've got a date, blondie. Don't tell me you've forgotten.'

Lillian, with the dazed look of a rabbit meeting the eyes of a stoat, unbuckled her safety-belt and stood up. Everything, everyone else, suddenly became unreal. In all the world there was no one except herself and this man intent upon revenge.

'That's right,' Slade said. His gun gave the order again, indicating the exit. 'We're getting out. Start moving.'

'No!' Genevieve caught at Lillian's wrist. 'Don't go! We can't help you out there!'

'You can't help her in here.' Slade aimed the gun at Sandy's head and held it there while Genevieve's hand fell away.

'That's better.' The gun barrel moved to prod

Lillian in the back. 'Keep moving.'

Carson turned and saw the coiled spring that was Paul Jarvis. 'Steady,' he said softly. 'Steady.'

Paul turned to meet the warning eyes. He shook his head, denying compromise, denying common sense. He could not sit by and let that *animal* take Lillian outside and –

'Steady,' Carson said again. His eyes seemed to be trying to signal something.

'That's right,' Slade said. He was opening the door now. 'Keep steady. I'll send your girl-friend back to you – when I've finished with her.'

Paul tensed and edged forward on his seat, but Slade caught the movement. The gun moved to cover him as the door slid open.

'Don't try it!' Slade said.

Sandy screamed again, her brief remission from pain ended. Genevieve tried to embrace her, but Sandy twisted away, still screaming.

'Think of the kid,' Slade said. 'You want to get her to a doctor, don't you? Just don't get funny and you can take off again as soon as we get out.'

'We're not leaving without Lillian,' Paul said steadily, speaking to Genevieve and Carson as much as to Slade. He was relieved to see that Genevieve nodded agreement.

'Have it your way,' Slade said magnanimously. 'We won't be long. I've got places to go. You can wait and take off then – as soon as she crawls back aboard.'

'Steady,' Carson said again, as Slade pushed Lillian out of the door and, with a final warning wave of his gun, leaped out after her.

But Paul was on his feet now, dodging away from

Genevieve's restraining hand. 'I can't let her go like that – ' He pushed past Genevieve. 'Don't you see – ?'

'*Oui.*' Genevieve turned back to Sandy, trying to soothe her child. 'You are right, *mon chéri*. We cannot leave her here. But hurry!'

Paul moved swiftly down the aisle, barely aware of anything but the open door of the aircraft. If he could reach it before Slade closed it . . . If only Slade would not think of closing it behind him . . .

'Jarvis!' He half-turned at the sound of Carson's voice, but all his attention was concentrated on the door. It remained open. Slade was not going to close it, then. Good. But . . . what did that portend for Lillian? Was Slade already wreaking his revenge – ?

'Jarvis,' Carson said urgently. 'Don't try to take him. He's got a gun *and* a knife.'

'He's got Lillian,' Paul said.

'All right. Get her if you can, and then come back here,' Carson said. 'We've still got a better chance in the aircraft than outside.'

Paul nodded. They'd all have a chance – once Slade had emptied his gun at an easy target.

'Keep low,' Carson said. 'Remember to keep low – and don't try to be a dead hero. Get the girl away from him and give me a shout when you've got her. But keep low – do you understand?'

Paul nodded again and plunged through the open doorway.

CHAPTER XXIX

It was like diving into solid cloud. So much so that his feet hit the ground with an impact as though he had stepped off an unexpected kerb. The ground had seemed much farther away.

Paul crouched low, trying to get some bearing. Overhead, the lazy churn of the rotor disturbed the mist but did nothing towards dispelling it. In the faint light from the open doorway behind him, Paul could see only the swirling mist and darker shadows that mocked him. Visibility: zero.

He heard a sob and moved in that direction, trying to be silent. But the ground was hillocky and uneven. He stumbled and heard a snarled curse ahead – Slade was not finding the going easy, either.

The clatter of the rotors was a reassuring point of reference in the enshrouding fog. Carson would keep the engines going as long as the fuel held out, ready to lift off quickly once they were aboard again. *If* they got aboard again.

Paul moved outward, still crouching low. He had to get away from the helicopter so that any shots he attracted would not accidentally hit the craft. Slade's gun was a Magnum, which meant that he ought to use both hands to aim it true, but while trying to hold on to Lillian, Slade had only one hand. That meant the kick from the gun would send the shot off-target. Not that it mattered that much with a Magnum – one of those bullets hitting you anywhere would stop you. It needn't

be through the heart. Paul flinched at the thought.
Then he heard Slade's voice, but not his words.
Lillian answered with another sob.

What was he saying to her? What was he doing to
her?

Paul moved in the direction of their voices, his
resolve strengthening.

'Slade!' he shouted. 'Slade, here I am!'

The silence ahead was suddenly as thick as the fog.

'Slade,' he called again. 'Slade, I'm coming after
you!'

If Slade had paused to reflect for a moment, he
would have recognized the hopeless bravado of the
threat. But Slade was on the run again – and with a
captive in tow.

'I'm coming, Slade!' He had to keep Slade's mind
off Lillian.

The shot rang out when he had stopped expecting it.
The bullet whizzed by unnervingly close to his ear.
Even one-handed, Slade was a better marksman than
he had thought.

'Go back, Paul!' Lillian called. 'He'll – ' She broke
off with a muffled scream.

Slade had still not moved very far from the aircraft.
He wouldn't, if he intended to shoot it down as it took
to the air again. But he had one bullet less to work with
now.

'You're finished, Slade!' Paul taunted, and crouched
quickly. *Keep low*, Carson had said, and it was good
advice. The next bullet passed over his head. Slade's
aim was too good. Perhaps it was time to stop making
such an obvious target of himself.

But two bullets were used up – and he was still alive.

More, he had not even been hit. Paul began to feel a rising confidence. Time for an old trick – what did he have to lose?

Paul pulled a handful of loose coins from his pocket and tossed them as far into the fog as he could. There came a muffled sound as they landed, followed immediately by another shot aimed in that direction. The coins had bought one more of Slade's bullets – money well spent.

The sobs from Lillian stopped abruptly, as though a hand had been clamped across her mouth and nostrils. Now there was silence, punctuated by the rhythmic clatter of the rotors in the background.

Paul moved sideways, still crouching. The land seemed to be sloping upwards, gradually at first, then more sharply, as though they were at the foot of a hill. Was that an additional reason why Slade had not moved too far away?

Sandy's screams could still be heard faintly. Each one twisted his nerves. He wanted to rush back to the aircraft and command it to take off immediately – let them take their chances with Slade's aim in the fog. But if he did, the next screams he heard would be Lillian's.

He had too many hostages to Fortune. And Fortune had turned her face away from him after having smiled upon him for so many years.

Or had she? His crablike progress was taking him in a wide circle around the aircraft, with a steep slope rising immediately behind. It seemed that the helicopter had come down in the centre of a bowl-shaped depression. A little more to one side in any direction and they would have crashed down on the hillside and turned turtle.

It was luck, or damned clever navigating on Carson's part. Perhaps both.

The silence seemed to be unnerving Slade. A random shot thudded uselessly into the hillside. How many more were left in the chamber of the gun?

Now Paul could discern footsteps immediately ahead. Uneven, stumbling footsteps, revealing the awkwardness of two people trying to move as one over the hummocks and hillocks of the rough terrain.

Even Slade must begin to realize that he could make faster progress on his own. But to let Lillian go would mean forfeiting an additional shield of protection, as well as his revenge. He was well beyond sanity, but how far beyond self-protection had his madness carried him?

Paul advanced steadily. Perhaps he had passed some unmarked bastion of sanity himself. He did not know. He knew only that he must tear Lillian from Slade's grasp before he could plan any other move.

A muffled curse as the pair ahead stumbled again. Another sob from Lillian was clearly audible. Slade must have withdrawn the hand covering her mouth in order to balance himself and prevent them from falling.

Now! Now – while Slade was off-balance and holding Lillian lightly!

Paul rushed at the shadows in the fog. He careered into them, snatching at the soft fabric his hands recognized as Lillian's jacket. He pulled at it and felt her begin to fight her captor, struggling to escape.

Taken off-guard, Slade battled to hold on. But they were both against him now. In the desperate tug-o'-war

Slade could not aim his gun. Another shot whistled past Paul.

'The next one is hers!' Slade panted, trying to set the muzzle of the gun against Lillian's neck. But she was wrenched from his grasp abruptly. The shot went wild. They fell, so suddenly had Lillian broken free of Slade's grip. Even as they hit the earth, Paul was urging her forward, pushing her head down. *Keep low.*

As they crawled towards the helicopter, Paul remembered Carson's warning and gave a short sharp shout.

'*Got her!*'

Inside the aircraft, Carson heard the signal he had been waiting for. He peered out into the fog and thought that he could discern movement low to the ground, with a dark tall form in mindless pursuit.

'Cross your fingers,' he said to Genevieve, and slammed his foot down heavily on the rudder panel.

The aircraft swivelled slowly as the tail rotor swung the aircraft in the familiar pivot.

The aircraft juddered as the tail rotor glanced off some soft obstacle. There was an anguished, abruptly cut-off cry . . . then silence. Even Sandy had stopped screaming.

'*Mon Dieu!*' Genevieve closed her eyes, her lips moved in silent prayer. She opened her eyes again and stared at Carson's uncompromising back. 'Did you do that deliberately?'

Carson turned and met her gaze. 'Do you care?'

Genevieve thought the question over carefully. 'Perhaps not.' She met his gaze levelly. 'Not if you got the right one.'

'I'll check that for you.' Carson left his seat and hurried past her. 'Also the rear rotor before we take off again. I don't *think* he did it any damage.'

Carson vanished through the doorway, leaving Genevieve staring after him, watching the open door breathlessly for what seemed like hours.

A small hand appeared in the doorway, broken once-elegant fingernails clawed for purchase. Then a golden head rose into sight. Ungracefully, Lillian was heaved up and through the doorway.

'It's all right,' Carson reported cheerfully, leaping aboard. 'We're still in business.'

'That's that.' Paul followed immediately behind, slamming the door shut as though the thing outside might still have the power to harm them. 'Can we get this machine to the nearest French city with a hospital?'

'Not likely,' Carson grinned at him. 'We'd do better to keep to the original plan and head for the Great Ormond Street Hospital. We're still in England.'

'England!' Genevieve breathed thankfully. 'How is it possible?'

'We turned back in mid-Channel.' Carson reached for the radio to report to Air Traffic Control and correct the original flight plan. 'Slade might have been good with a blade, but he was bloody awful with any sort of direction finder.'

'Can we make it?' Paul asked anxiously, as the helicopter rose into the air. Sandy lay so still, so silent. 'We're on the emergency fuel supply, aren't we?'

The engines coughed, then purred as the rotors lifted them above the fog.

'We are now,' Carson said.

*

The floodlights of Coram's Fields blazed a golden welcome beneath the pinkish-black dawn sky of London. As the Sikorsky settled down in a soft landing, they could see the ambulance waiting just beyond the rim of light.

'I'm sorry we can't come with you –' Paul apologized. 'But the Board – '

'It's all right,' Genevieve said. 'Of course you must save your Company. We understand.' Her gaze went beyond him.

'I'll telephone as soon as the meeting is over,' Paul promised. But already his thoughts were moving ahead. Even after he and Lillian had cleaned themselves up as much as possible, they were going to make a pretty dramatic entrance. There would be no time to change and they were begrimed and faintly splattered with blood. By now, the police would have located Slade's body and the early news reports would be filtering out to the general public. Those of the Board with the best sources of information would already know the position. Undoubtedly Harlow would leak the news to the others.

That alone might be enough to turn the tide. It would prove that Paul Jarvis was still a winner. And everybody wanted to be associated with a winner. Especially in the City.

Carson left his seat and went to help the ambulance men with Sandy. Paul and Lillian drew back slightly as he approached Genevieve.

'I'll come back as soon as I've dropped these two,' Carson said.

'It isn't necessary,' Genevieve said. 'They'll operate immediately, I think. It may take some time.'

'Then I'll wait with you,' Carson said. 'Someone should – and the boss has his hands full.'

'That's very kind of you.' She tucked the blankets around Sandy, not looking up.

'It's not all kindness,' Carson admitted. 'I've developed an ulterior motive. Do you mind?'

'No.' Genevieve glanced up at him demurely. 'I don't mind. I'd rather hoped you had.'

If you have enjoyed this book and would like to receive details of other Walker mystery titles, please write to:

Mystery Editor
Walker and Company
720 Fifth Avenue
New York, NY 10019